T0063381

MBIRAMATAKO

Kant Mbiramatako

PARTRIDGE
A Penguin Random House Company

To order additional copies of this book, contact
Toll Free 800 101 2657 (Singapore)
Toll Free 1 800 81 7340 (Malaysia)
orders.singapore@partridgepublishing.com

www.partridgepublishing.com/singapore

ACKNOWLEDGEMENTS

Godmother, you made it happen, my entire family,
June, you always special,

CHAPTER 1

'Today we have, today we have, ohm.' I was dumbstruck. I stood in front of the school assembly. From first grade to the seventh grade. We were celebrating Commonwealth day. At my school each class was required to do a drama play themed towards the Commonwealth. The best acts were picked to present at morning assembly. Our class act was impressive. The first part involved introducing the topic of our presentation. I was chosen to ace that part. During rehearsals I acted brilliantly. The crucial moment I crumbled. I could not say a word. The whole act had to abandon performance. My colleagues were furious. My teacher was boiling with disappointment. One girl, Beauty confronted me. Before I knew it, punch! I clearly remember seeing stars. I staggered but did not fall. I didn't fight her back. I was shaky from the experience. That was my first time face to face with embarrassment. I never wanted to experience it again.

My name is Mbiramatako. I was born in May of '76. I was born a big bubbly boy with all three hundred bones intact. In adulthood I have two hundred and six. Others have fused as I have grown. Everyone was happy that time. The cool winds of May blew fresh in my sweet little face! On the day of my birth my mom swung me in her arms. She sang a very famous song called 'We don't have a home on this earth.' It sounded strange for neighbours and others who heard her celebrate my birth with a song normally sang at funerals! Mom understood very well the close affinity between creation and death. Blood was shed daily in the liberation struggle. She was afraid of death like every mother. She confronted it. I guess that freed her form the fear. Familiarity breeds contempt. My eldest sister remembers that time as the rare time when there was real harmony in my family. That time my father ceased drinking. Mom always got her Fanta orange after dinner.

I'd entered a nervous world. In my country a war was drawing to a close. The atmosphere was charged. Politics, party clashes and the heady feeling of impending victory. My uncle Tony in later years told me that the nationalists were airing broadcasts from neighbouring Mozambique. He imitated the authoritarian voice of the broadcaster, 'people of Zimbabwe, victory is certain.' Indeed victory was certain. Victory over the imperialist who brought the three Cs, Christianity, commerce and civilisation years before to my country. Why were we fighting him? He dangled the three Cs and took our wealth and freedoms to self govern. That year the first email was done in March. Queen Elizabeth II sent out the first royal email from the Royal Signals and Radar Establishment. Today when I surf the net and open my Tumblr account, twit or facebook with friends, it never occurs to me that the internet was first made for military purposes. Technology continues to improve. There is the ipad, iphone and the Google glasses. The glasses are worn like normal spectacles. They're described in a local daily newspaper as having internet, can take photos and video short snippets. Google the company behind the glasses say that the glasses are 'seamless and empowering. They will have the ability to capture any chance encounter, from a celebrity sighting to a grumpy salesclerk, and broadcast it to millions in seconds.'

My family was in joyful bliss. The world was restless. That year alone America tested nuclear arsenal from January to December a record 10 times! Russia, then known as USSR was in direct competition with the US. China tested nuclear weapons three times! France performed nuclear test in '76. In April of that year, US and Russia agreed on the size of nuclear tests for peaceful use. I came into a threatened world. Fast-forward thirty seven years.

Nuclear arsenal is still the most malign threat to existence. Currently there is a lot of war rhetoric concerning Iran and North Korea. The two countries claim their rights to enhance nuclear agility. The US and its allies stand firm. Reasoning that it's too risky to trust nuclear weapons in the clutches of 'rogue countries.' Acts of aggression are fuelled by apparent prospects of peace and security. Wars never build anything that peace cannot.

The first Martian landing in history happened in 1976. US Viking 1 landed on Mars. Viking 1 radio signal from Mars proved general theory of relativity. Thirty seven years later, enter Curiosity Mars rover. A much more sophisticated project to find out if there was life on planet Mars. The world's largest telescope (600cm) became operational by USSR in '76. Today there are more advanced telescopes like the Hubble telescope. It has taken spectacular pictures of deep space. Despite massive improvements in science and technology humans are still clueless about the mystery of life. The brilliance of science cannot be denied. Science discovers what God has given to us in puzzle form. Science decodes the intricacies of life.

In January of 1976, Sara Jane Moore was sentenced to life for trying to shoot Pres Ford. The 11th director of the CIA in 1976 was George Bush. He later became president of the US from January 2001 to January 2009. He had one of the worst terms in US history. He presided over wars in Iraq and in Afghanistan. During his term the US was attacked in what is known as the 9/11 attacks. Jimmy Carter Democratic candidate defeated Gerald Ford Republican for president. In his term as president, the Shah of Iran was kicked from power. Ayatollah came to power. The American people kidnappings happened. President Carter ended his term still struggling to get hostages out of Iran. Playboy later released Jimmy Carter's interview that he lusts for women.

Chinese politburo fires vice Premier Deng Xiaoping. Mao tse Tung and Richard Nixon held their final meeting in '76. Mao Zedong's funeral took place in Beijing. Hua Guo-feng succeeded

Mao Tse-tung as chairman of Communist Party. In March of 1976 British premier Harold Wilson resigned as James Callaghan became PM of England.

Christopher Ewart-Biggs British ambassador to the Republic of Ireland was assassinated by the Provisional IRA. 10,000 Northern Ireland women demonstrate for peace in Belfast. As I grew up IRA was always in the news about bombings. IRA was formed in 1922. Great Britain ruled Ireland around the 18th century to about 1921. Irish separatists launched a violent guerrilla war on them. Sinn Fein the separatists' political party signed the Anglo Irish treaty which gave full independence to 26 counties in the south. Britain retained control of six counties in the north. A civil war exploded between supporters of the treaty and anti treaty groups. The Anti treaty group formed IRA. Car bombs, kidnappings, extortion, beatings and assassinations were carried out against British police and military in Ireland and in Great Britain. This was done as a way to demand the unification of all 32 counties in Ireland by IRA. A ceasefire was finally announced by IRA in 1994. In 1998 the Good Friday agreement was reached. IRA took a peaceful way in their quest for a united Ireland. Sometimes violent tendencies sporadically erupt.

In that year, 1976, there was a failed coup in Niger. One American and three British mercenaries were executed in Angola following the Luanda Trial. Egypt president Sadat was re-elected in the middle of that year. Seychelles gained independence from Britain.

In Vietnam elections were held in April of 1976. The aim was for a national assembly to reunite the country. Formal reunification of North and South Vietnam was done in June of 1976. Vietnam was ruled by France for six decades before Japan joined in by invading parts of Vietnam in 1940. Revolutionary leader Ho Chi Minh set up the Viet Minh to clear Vietnam of the French and Japanese. In 1950 the US came in to help France to fight the Viet Minh. They desired to stop the communist influence which Viet Minh represented. In 1954 the French pulled out after the Viet Minh kicked their back sides at Dien Bien Phu. In 1956 a general election was imminent to unite Vietnam. The US disagreed to an election in fear of communist victory. South Vietnam did an election in the South only. Ngo Dinh Diem was elected. He was brutal. The national liberation front known as the Viet Cong was started in 1960. It booted out Ngo Dinh Diem. The US sent more advisers to Vietnam amidst war between Viet Cong and South Vietnamese in the south. In the north the Viet Minh were active. They attacked two US ships in international waters. Lyndon Johnson got approval to send ground troops to Vietnam in 1965. The protracted Vietnamese war had started. In 1973 the US left Vietnam without managing to plug communism. Vietnam was unified under communism. Vietnam is peaceful and progressive without foreign interference.

Indonesian president Suharto annexed East Timor in 1976. Japanese ex-premier Tanaka was arrested in the Lockheed Affair. Argentine President Isabel Peron was deposed by the country's military in June.

Court martial began in USSR for Valeri Sablin. He was a Captain 3rd rank. He was accused of seizing the ship Storozhevoy. He confined the ship's captain and other officers to the wardroom. Sablin planned to go to Leningrad. He wished to address the nation about the corruption of the authorities. He was captured and shot dead by Russian authorities. Tom Clancy wrote a novel in 1984 based on this incident called Hunt for Red October. It was made into a movie in 1990 starring Sean Connery.

My dad was a great fan of boxing. He talked of boxers like George Foreman and Muhammad Ali. In January of the year I was born, George Foreman knocked out Ron Lyle in fifth round. The fight was described as a real slugfest. Muhammad Ali knocked out Jan Pierre Coopman in fifth round in a fight for heavyweight boxing title. He went on to win against, Jimmy Young, Richard Dunn and Ken Norton in 1976 alone. Earlier Ali had been involved in a dispute with the US government when he refused to be drafted into the army to fight in the Vietnam War. This almost cost him his career but he made a comeback in the seventies. Ali is now into philanthropy. In 1984 he told the world about his Parkinson disease. He founded the Muhammad Ali Parkinson centre in Phoenix, Arizona. He is in support of various charity missions including the Special Olympics and the make a wish foundation. He received the presidential Medal of Freedom from President George Bush in 2005. One favourite saying from Muhammad Ali is, 'A man who views the world the same at fifty as he did at twenty has wasted thirty years of his life.'

In football Bayern Munich wins twenty first Europe cup. Liverpool won fifth UEFA cup at the bridge. In June of 1976, Czechoslovakia becomes European soccer champs. It has not won again since that year. Modern football was built in Britain, England around 1863. The union des associations europeenennes de football, UEFA is the body responsible for football in Europe. It was formed in 1954 in Basel, Switzerland. In tennis, Wimbledon Men's Tennis, Bjorn Borg beats Ilse Nastase. Bjorn Borg says that, 'It's tough when you're No. 1. You don't have any private life, you can't even walk anywhere. I think that was one reason why I lost my motivation to play tennis.' He retired in 1984. In his short career he won 11 Grand Slam titles. He is ranked fourth among male players who won the grand slam. He made millions in his career.

In Olympics, the opening of the Summer Olympics is marred by 25 African teams boycotting the New Zealand team. The African countries were against the international Olympic committee's refusal to ban New Zealand for touring apartheid South Africa for a rugby tournament.

In the US, OJ Simpson gains 273 yards for Buffalo vs. Detroit. He stopped football in 1979 and began an acting career. In 1994 OJ was involved in a gruesome tale. Accused of murdering his ex wife Nicole Brown Simpson and boyfriend Ron Goldman. He escaped jail sentence in what became known as the trial of the century. In 2006 Simpson wrote a book of a hypothetical scene of how he would have killed Nicole and Ron. He planned to publish it but the deal was not successful. The book was called 'if I did it'. A bankruptcy judge gave the rights to the book to Goldman's family who retitled it to 'if I did it; confessions of the killer'. OJ got incarcerated for years for robbing two sports memorabilia dealers at gunpoint in a Las Vegas hotel room.

In music on the international scene, The Beatles released their LP 'Rock & Roll Music'. The Beatles' musical career is legendary and they are the best selling act in history. EMI records approximate sales in the billions by the Beatles to date. They featured in Time magazine's selection of the 20th century's 100 most influential people. They won seven Grammy awards in their career. Sid Berstein offered $230 million charity concert for Beatle reunion.

George Harrison was doing well outside the Beatles. He later got into trouble for plagiarism. In February of 1976 he released 'This Guitar can't keep from Crying'. In April George Harrison sang lumberjack song with Monty Python. He released "This Song". In August of the same year, George Harrison was found guilty of plagiarizing "My Sweet Lord" In the later part of 1976, the US courts found George Harrison guilty of plagiarism for the song, 'He's So Fine'. He died of cancer in 2001. He had a successful career in solo recordings and film production. George Harrison had soul. He was involved in charity work. He teamed up with Bob Dylan, Leon Russell and Ravi Shankar. They organised concerts at Madison square garden to aid refugees in Bangladesh. They amassed $ 15 million in donation to UNICEF. At the same time they did a Grammy winner of an album.

In the USA, Queen's Bohemian Rhapsody' went gold. Queen's lead singer was Freddie mercury. He was born in Tanzania in Zanzibar. His real name was Farookh Bulsara. He went to school in India. Later his family moved to UK. Freddie was bisexual and lived lavishly. He loved champagne and art. In years to come, Freddie became ill. In 1991 he announced that he had full blown AIDS. He died the next day.

In December of 1976 Bob Marley survived a hit on him and his family in a politically motivated move. This happened two days before a concert. Bob went ahead and played. He fled Jamaica the next day. He was awarded the Order of Merit by the Jamaican government. He received the Medal of Peace from the United Nations in 1980. He sold more than twenty million records in his career. Marley l died of cancer in Miami, Florida on May 11 1981.

In the same year, 1976 Allman Brother's roadie Scooter Herring was sentenced to 75 years for providing drugs for the group. This was based on Gregg Allman's testimony. Gregg later fled to Los Angeles. In 1977 he released an album with his wife, Cher. In the same year, 1976 rock group Deep Purple disbands. They are from England. They were listed in the Guinness book of world records as the loudest band for a concert in London in 1972. They sold over a hundred million album sales all over the world. The group went through line-up changes. It is still there today.

The eighteenth Grammy Awards were held in 1976. Natalie Cole won with, 'Love Will Keep Us Together.' Grammy awards were originally referred to as Gramophone Award. Sometimes simply referred to as Grammys. The national academy of recording arts and sciences of the US are behind the Grammys. May is a lucky month for me. I was born in May and the Grammys also! The first ceremony was held in May of 1959. The 55th Grammy ceremony was held in 2013.

Business at Walt Disney was already rolling. In March of '76 they logged in their 50 millionth guests. On the international economic scene Britain was performing below par. The British pound fell below $2 for the first time. In Washington D C things were looking up. They opened an underground metro. Wozniak and Steven Jobs founded apple computer. In the US the first apple I pad was created. In the aviation industry great strides continued to be made. Pan Am began non stop flights New York to Tokyo. The first commercial SST flight flew from US to North America. Concorde flew to Washington DC. Arabic Monetary Fund was established in Abu Dhabi in April of 1976. The rollercoaster revolution made of steel with a vertical flip opens at Six Magic Mountain. Canada CCN Tower in Toronto opened at 555m. It became the tallest free standing structure. Mexican peso was devalued. Metro liner was officially opened in Brussels.

In international crime women were taking part in action. Newspaper heiress Patricia Hearst was sentenced to 7 years for a 1974 bank robbery. She was later released after 22 months by President Carter. In the US the Supreme Court rules that death penalty is not intrinsically mean or unusual. Utah Supreme Court gave the go ahead for the execution of convicted murderer Gary Gilmore. Human right issues were in focus. In March of 1976 International Bill of Rights went into effect. 35 nations ratified it. Kenneth Gibson became 1st black president of US conference of Mayors. Mary Langdon became 1st British firewoman. First woman was admitted to Air Force Academy in Colorado Springs Colo. Episcopal Church approved ordination of women as priests and bishop in 1976. Amnesty International received Erasmus-prize. Transsexual Renee Richards was barred from competing in US Tennis Open. Nobel Prize for chemistry was awarded to William N Lipscomb Jr. American Saul Bellow won Nobel Prize for Literature. Minister Irene Vorrink began fluoridating Dutch drinking water.

1976 had its fair share of anguish. Natural disasters happened in Friuli situated in Italy, causing 989 deaths and the destruction of entire villages. 8.2 Tangshan earthquake killed an estimated 240,000 Chinese. An earthquake and tidal wave in the Philippines killed up to 8,000. Heavy earthquake struck China, 1,000s die. Two airliners collide over Yugoslavia and kill all 176 aboard. A Bolivian Boeing 707 cargo jet crashes in Santa Cruz, 70 die as Norwegian tanker Frosta collides with George Prince. Train collision at Goes Neth, 7 die. Death and destruction, leaving people in dire straits. But there was glimmer of hope, one heroic act by Shavarsh Karapetyan, who saved 20 people from the trolleybus that had fallen into Erevan reservoir.

Israel launched rescue of Air France crew and passengers being held at Entebbe Airport by pro Palestinian hijackers. Uganda asked UN to condemn Israeli hostage rescue raid on Entebbe. Christian militia conquer Palestinian camp Tell al-Za'tar, 2000 people were killed. Palestinians hijack KLM DC-9 to Cyprus. Five Croatian terrorists captured TWA-plane at La Guardia Airport, NY. Battle of Aishiya in Lebanon is fought. Syrian army conquerors Beirut. The Chimpanzee is placed on the List of Endangered Species.

Nearer home Mozambique closed its border with Zimbabwe in March. Race riot in Cape Town South Africa resulted in 17 people dead. South Africa decided to allow multi-racial teams to represent them. UN General Assembly condemns apartheid in South Africa. Angola was admitted to UN. Anti apartheid advocate Dumisa Ntsebeza was arrested in South Africa in Soweto. South Africa student uprisings began in what is now recognised as 'Soweto Day'.

In four years time my country got independence from Ian Smith's government. Robert Marley was formally invited by the new republic. The government did not have enough money for the invite. Bob sponsored it and jetted into the excited atmosphere of victory celebration. Bob Marley penned a song for the country called 'Zimbabwe', which goes, 'everybody got a right to decide their own destiny, no more internal power struggles, soon we will find out who is the real revolutionary?' What great prophecy and vision. The revolution was about land. The war was won. The greatest expectation was that land would go to the people. That was not to be. People reading headlines of newspapers that year never thought the country would be in shambles so soon after independence. Politicians with selfish tendencies forgot the people. They went on a rampage of wealth amassment.

In the years that followed independence the real goings on were confusing. Especially to ordinary civilians like me. Government was very sensitive with information. I'm amazed to realise that for thirty plus years of my life I've known only one President. No wonder my country is in doldrums. One man ruling for so long means that his mistakes certainly balloon into disaster for the nation. As fierce and dictatorial as he is, it's not his fault that my country has sunk. It's my fault and each and every Zimbabwean's fault. Bad things happen if good people do nothing about it. The main reason there was no change in my country's politics can be attributed to the Zimbabwean people who managed to scrounge and amass enough riches and influence to feel comfortable with the status quo. The exploitation of the common man is the same.

One stand up comedian said Michael Jackson discovered that the nose he really wished to have was a white nose. After surgery he discovered that a white nose just didn't look good on a nigger's face. He went on to remedy the cheek bones in order to suit the white nose. He kept amending his face until it became a stranger's face on him. The moral of this is a painful reality that the oppressed people always aspire to be like their tormentors. Our leaders act exactly as the oppressors did. Problem is they are not good imitators. They leave people exposed to poverty. The oppressors before were good at looking after their people. In the eighties or nineties, Ian Smith made newspaper headlines when he challenged my President to walk in First Street and see who got attacked by the people. People don't need old rhetoric about the legacy of colonialism. Certainly people do not need violence. People need not patriotism either. A lot of people were maimed and murdered in patriotic fervour. My government is in love with Machiavelli. He is the political philosopher who believed that lying is ok as long as it brings political objectives. The threat of the old colonialists is long gone. What remains is an illusion used as a tool to cajole people with and to justify oppression! Isn't it ironic?

People in my country achieved independence after an armed struggle. They literary took over. Parents were proud that their children were able to attend former white only elite schools. Workers found themselves employed in high rise offices enjoying the rituals of tea breaks and lunch. Donning jacket and tie and shopping in First Street. The flame of hope and aspiration died right there. People didn't challenge the former white schools by shunning them. They could build their own more elitist schools. This is achievement. From there everything else should have been done better than previously.

Most African countries are in the same state. In my country the roads left by the colonialists has been patched for thirty plus years. Is it good economics or stupidity? The money to pave new roads will be available. Someone high up will pocket some and patch the road with the balance. This is common knowledge but people do nothing about it.

My father's mother was as strong as my mothers' mother, grandma Chihwiza. She had strong influence. She wasn't satisfied with her daughter in law. She wished her son to find another wife. The son did not look for another wife. He continued with his choice. I never saw my grandma. If I did I do not recollect. I only heard stories about her. Dark stories. I was told that physically she was not a great looker. When I was born father stopped drinking. Granny was very cross. She boarded a bus to town. She confronted father on why he stopped drinking. Before she left they shared a mug of beer. Father enjoyed it and continued to for the rest of his life. She visited our house in town. After everyone had slept granny woke up. She opened the family mealie meal pack and put some juju inside. My eldest brother witnessed this. Another popular story about her was the one she sent her daughter's son to collect mom's panties. She wanted to use them for juju. The son collected it and delivered to her. It's very hard to conceal the head of a goat inside a paper packaging. The truth came out. The darkest story about grandma concerned my grandfather. My grandfather was said to be a very quiet man. He was short and handsome. He was a cook by profession. It was rumoured that there was a love triangle. Granny had a boyfriend. Grandfather was found hung inside the toilet. He allegedly hung himself. His sons and other relatives disputed. They argued that the noose was not strong enough. They alleged grandfather was standing with his feet on the ground. Foul play was strongly suspected. The police closed the case as suicide. Later in life my father's sister's daughter committed suicide. Her father was very strict. It was rumoured she became pregnant. She was in secondary school. She chose to take her own life than face her ferocious father. My father's sister committed suicide by drinking poison. I went to hospital to see her. She suffered a lot. She was talking. She looked like she was going to recover. She talked to me and asked about my mother. We left her at night. Before we reached home the hospital called. She had passed on.

I was four years old when the first big fight between mom and dad happened. It's vague in my memory but I remember that fight. Me being passed on to mom by dad through the bedroom window. Mom put me on her back. We went to father's relatives in a nearby suburb. We put up for the night there. The rest I'm not clear. It resulted in mom taking the whole family to our grandmother's farm. I was not yet going to school. My brother and two sisters were. They were uprooted and taken to grandma's farm. Grandma Chihwiza was a very strong willed woman. She was educated to basic level. At an early age she left my infant mom with her mother. She went to work in the city before she suddenly packed everything and returned to her village. She settled at the nearby farm which belonged to the white man.

She invaded a big portion of the farm. Grandma was the pioneer of land invasions. She showed that she was indigenous to the land. She was entitled to it when necessity demanded. The land invasions that were later carried out were politically crafted in haste to save an imminent fall from power. The invasions were to spite the so called outside political influence. It was a sham of a programme. The ruling party manifesto recognises land as the most fundamental resource. I'm surprised that they went on to tear and ravage the precious resource in the name of land reform. The chaotic land reform resulted in rampant damage to natural flora and fauna. Even in the urban areas where no land reform was taking place. Small bands of men under the guise of the party went after natural wind breaks and open areas. They cut trees for resale as firewood. Firewood was in demand because of the problem of electricity. The patches of land were better off when we did urban farming. My family supplemented corn from the patches. We grew Sweet potatoes for breakfast on the patches of land. We never indiscriminately cut down trees. The land finally went to the people but at great cost both to the land and the common man like me who got nothing from the land reform.

The place that grandma Chihwiza chose was sacred. The white farmer was not planting there. The white man used to pay homage to that sacred place. He brought clothe and beads as offerings. My grandma was the only human inhabiting there. She had no food, no shelter. Grandma Chihwiza claims she survived under spiritual duress until the white farmer brought her corn. She roasted it and drank water. The area was special. Grandma built three huts without doors. We stayed in these huts without doors yet nothing bad happened to us! She built a stone wall around the homestead. Grandma could manipulate nature to help her. The homestead grew under her ownership. Villagers used to come for consultations and traditional rites. The area had lush green vegetation, closely growing trees and huge granite stones. There was one particularly long granite stone that rose like a tower high into the sky. It was an amazing eerie place, scary. Wild animals roamed that area. The area was very susceptible to lightning. Sometimes it was so intense we could see trees being struck right next to the homestead. It never struck inside the homestead. Sometimes mom ululated in terror as bolt after bolt of lightning hit. The clap of thunder moments after deafening us. It seemed to go on for a long time before there was just the sound of the raindrops. Peace at last. The birds came out of hiding and start tooting and chirping.

In my culture when too much blood is spilt, the forces of nature can erupt in potent anger. This force can manifest in anyone to help to stop the bloodshed. The spirits of my ancestors unleashed in all their powerful splendour in grandma. She was a smouldering fire. High with the spirit. My sister remembered the day she came to our house in town. Neighbours were spiteful. Some scolded in their minds but to everyone's surprise grandma repeated their thoughts aloud in their tone of voice! She never took tape water. Grandma used to take snuff tobacco. At times she went for days without eating. Grandma Chihwiza meditated for long days, making continuous noises from her throat in repetitive patterns. Sometimes she sat under an indigenous tree and chanted the whole day. When the war became very hot she did not eat. Just stood facing eastwards with snuff in hand and chant and chant. Days after that there were reports of a fierce battle between the nationalists and the settler forces.

Most of the young men who went to join the war first came to consult grandma. They were cleansed and prepared for war. They came back to the farm at Independence to pay homage to grandma. The new President of the country sent delegates for consultations. She was powerful. More so to my mother. The delegates were sent from what became known as number 88. I remember all the interesting and colourful characters. They were former combatants fresh from war. They came with tape recorders and they recorded grandma. They took the recordings to the Prime Minister. There used to be big ceremonies where mbira, a traditional music instrument, was played backed up by congas and singing. Some became possessed and rolled on the ground. It used to be an exciting chaos when the nationalists visited. One of them wanted to marry my sister but it did not suffice.

In 1981–82 there was a severe drought. I witnessed this from innocent eyes. The villagers came and gathered at the farm. A rain dance ceremony was done. Before it was over a dark cloud settled above the Muchakata tree where the ceremony was being held. Bolts of lightning and thunder and heavy rain fell. People never ran for cover. They continued most jerking awkwardly about in the deep throes of spiritual possession. I witnessed this miracle done by grandma Chihwiza, with my own eyes.

At granny's farm it was forbidden to eat sugar. Or use commercial tea leaves. We used a local variety called Zumbani. No iron or silverware for cooking and eating. No perfume. The diet was strict. Everything we ate we produced and processed it right there at her farm. Sometimes food got scarce especially during the dry season. Most remarkably, it was in the thick of wild bush but we were never harmed. Snakes used to perch up in my grandma's hut. We witnessed spectacular fights between snakes and chameleons. In the heat of the summer, we slept outside looking up at the vast sky full of twinkling stars.

The golden weaver or Jesa in local dialect was the most melodious of all birds. It made the homestead alive with its endless energy! It was very good at crafting exquisite nests at the Checheni tree nearby. Jesa is yellow and grey in colour. The male more brightly coloured, the eyes and beak darker. It's the one that did the weaving and the singing. There was one tiny type of bird that I fell in love with. It was blue in colour. In local dialect it is called Dhimba. During the rainy season food was abundant at Chihwiza farm. We caught succulent flying ants. In the Mopani trees we harvested Mopani worms. At night we roasted fresh corn, sweet as if applied sugar. Sugar was forbidden at the farm. Grandma used to make pumpkin pudding in the morning. A mixture of pumpkin mashed together with peanut butter and cooked over the wood fire, the pot steadfastly balanced on three medium sized stones. That was the fireplace we ever used.

There was a man who came for treatment at the farm. He stayed with us for a whole month. He was very skilled at trapping mice. I used to set my traps around the farm. I didn't have the skill and good luck as this man. At times my trap remained set with the bait carefully eaten by the mice! One early morning I went to check my traps. I collected the mice in my traps plus from the other man's traps and took them home. Mom took a look at them. As much as we all loved delicious mice, she was startled by the number. 'Where did you get them?' She asked. I hesitated. She knew immediately. 'Go and put the mice back right now and go dig a small hole and spit in it and say you wont steal again!' I was afraid. Mom seldom became angry with me. She doted on me! I went and put the mice back. I knew stealing was prohibited but I was going to try it again later on.

The other prominent visitor to the farm was light skinned and sturdy on his feet. He was burly and short. He worked for the police force. He always came to help at the farm. When he walked the ground resonated with his footsteps. I assisted him to build a new hut to accommodate the swelling number of people visiting the farm. It was exciting. My first time to build a hut from scratch. We worked hard because he wanted to finish and rush for duty. I remember very well his voice coming from the top of the roof of the hut. He kept calling, 'grass Mbiramatako! Grass Mbiramatako!' By the end of it I was exhausted. He pushed me hard.

Three forces were at play in my family. One force prevailed and kept everything together. It manifested through a young girl. My elder sister. Subtle is our true God. The most powerful force was grandma Chihwiza due to the power of her spirit. The neutral force was my father. He was a hard man who went on with life the way he deemed fit. He never listened to anyone. He was above any expectations based on human feelings. There was something peculiar about my father. When he received shocking news, for example when his mother passed on, he went back into bed, took a newspaper and started reading! He let mom swing to and fro, never making a decisive drastic action like divorce her. I guess he understood she was confused. I attribute much of the confusion on conflicting systems of worship imposed on the people. Mom was confused between the modern view, or catholic and the traditional practice which grandma Chihwiza advocated for. She strived to keep a modern family that went to the local Roman Catholic Church. Like all young families did at that time. On the other hand she knew and felt the power of grandma's spirit. She had faith in it.

I don't blame mom. I felt the great love that she had for us. Mom fiercely defended her little one on a bus journey across the country. A trip to deep down eastern region. Near the border with Mozambique. Grandma had the knack for sudden journeys. Any particular journey she announced had to happen. No matter how far. On this occasion I dressed in my Sunday best. It used to be long trousers. It was pale green in colour. As Christmas after Christmas passed the backside gave in and was torn. Mom was very ingenious. She cut cloth from one of the trouser leg. Levelled it with the other and used the cloth to patch the backside. The ingenuity was repeated each time the backside gave in. By the time of this particular journey there was a heavy patch on my bum. The trouser was now shorts. On the bus I must have presented quite a picture with Grandma Chihwiza in tour. She was wearing her all black clothe tied around in traditional style, sporting dreadlocks. A middle aged man in a brown suit chose to push me away when I attempted to seat beside him. Alas, he had made a mistake. Mom was upon him in an instant. She clutched him with considerable amount of force. She shook him like a yellow lemon tree. The whole bus was noisy. We moved to another seat. It is better to face a wild animal than a protective mother.

Grandma had a white cat which she seemed to control psychically. She claimed that the cat had power to sense evil people. I remember that if grandma Chihwiza became cross with you. By the end of that week the cat would attack you with its nails. Several times that cat used to attack people. I was afraid of that fiery cat. There was a time grandma gave us a charmed stick to put underground on the yard. We dug and buried it. This happened when one of the man staying with us who was having an episode of psychiatric illness, was not around. When he came back he went straight to the sport where we had put the charm and he took it out. It's still a wonder to me how he knew it was there. Grandma always warned us about the white people's God which came through Catholicism.

At times grandma would disappear into the thick bushes around the farmstead. She came back with fresh bark from the Musasa tree. She proceeds to tie each and every child around. She would tie at the fore head, waist and chest. As the bark dries it contracts and tightens. It became painful as each day passed. We slept with it because it was prohibited to take it off on our own. The ordeal would go on until it ruptured on its own. Sometimes granny felt pity and removed it. She threw it in the nearby river. Often the last tattered shirt would be thrown together with the old bark. Granny will give a brisk bath. Afterwards I felt fresh minus my last shirt. We never used to visit any relatives at all except my grandma. Grandma is an unsung hero who deserves some worthy mention. Her legend just died.

When the family finally went back home, after some concerned relative intervened, father welcomed us! Mom stayed at the farm. My brother and sisters resumed school. Their counterparts were ahead. The headmaster agreed to jump my sister higher if she passed an entrance exam. It was heart wrenching to watch her in an old uniform she had worn earlier. Barefoot and very small for her age. The headmaster felt human welling of pity. Fortunately she passed the test! School resumed. She won even when odds were against her. The problem with mom's absence was there was freedom for everyone. Father brought the local prostitute. My eldest brother cohabitated with his girlfriend five years older than him.

CHAPTER 2

My eldest brother was intelligent. As soon as he completed 'O' levels he got an apprenticeship as a mechanic. That time it had just been opened up to Africans. It was prestigious. He did his with the National brewery in the country. They got the same benefits like workers there. They got two crates of beer each month. Those who did not drink gave at discount price to friends who drank. A lot of beer was around. It was endless party at the house. My father let out some rooms to get extra cash. The tenants were all male bachelors. They brought their female friends over. Amidst all the confusion there was one lone influence of reason. She kept everything together. She was so young anyone could have taken advantage. But she was a dangerous cat aware of what went on. Harrison, one of the male tenants tried to introduce his friend. He told him to ask her what shoe size she wore. She told him straight away to get lost. He was stunned. She is a strong character.

My entire family had nothing except her. A lot could have gone wrong at crucial moments in our lives. She always saved the day. She became the bridge between us the kids and all the new moms that father brought. She naturally became friends with them. I know it hurt her so much. I sometimes wonder how she absorbed so much pain. She had a small body. Father brought one woman from the pub. I was fast asleep. I didn't hear them come in. What woke me up was my sister sobbing. She was trying not to wake us up. She didn't cry easily. It had hurt her. Father came and asked her what she wanted him to do? Mom was not there. She was in form three that time. She's my Godmother.

Those days the community nurses were diligent in their work. They rounded schools to weigh the kids and check for immunization. My closest brother was found severely underweight. They wrote a letter to my parents. The nurses later made a follow up. They knocked at the front door. My sister opened for them. They could see obvious signs of an absent mother. They had noticed that the house did not have curtains. It had whitewash painted on the windows. The whitewash looked old so they could tell that was basically the curtaining. All sat on the sofa and asked where mom was. My sister told them she ran to the farm. They asked several other questions and referred the case to social welfare. No one followed up. Most of my young life I constantly faced food shortages. People fought for bread and mealie meal. The fight for bread became tragic. My second sister was pushed in a stampede for bread. The glass counter gave way. It crashed and made several cuts on her legs. She got stitches and anti tetanus injection at the local clinic.

We were playing at the patch of ground near my house. This was our soccer field. It was around 5 pm. The woman currently staying with dad called us. She said dinner was ready. We washed our hands at the tap outside entered and sat on the floor. She sat on the sofa and watched us eat. The dinner consisted of sadza/ ugali and fried vegetable. As we ate she commented on us. She went, 'that one is greedy, look how he opens his big mouth!' It was a very uncomfortable dinner. She made us hurry. She wanted to go to the local pub early. Before father finished work to join her. Her face was white with Pond's vanishing cream and powder. The lips painted red. After she went to the pub we rushed to our neighbour's house to watch television. Televisions later flooded and every household owned one. Earlier television sets were rare. Only a few households owned one. Every kid was intrigued by the box. One neighbour was kind. She allowed us to watch popular programmes through her front window. If she allowed us inside the house would be full of smelly unwashed kids!

The few relatives that I knew were the ones who used to visit us at home. They were few indeed! It was like our family was under sanctions. I was confused. My cousin brother was one of the few regular visitors. He came in two cars with his wife and kids. As the years went by my father became unemployed. He later got a job as a bar man with the local council. In the beginning my father and mother were devout Catholics. They wedded in church. All my siblings and me were baptised in church. My mom continued to go to church with other women. Her mom's influence would confuse her. She ended mixing Catholicism and voodoo.

Every one I grew up with knew ours was a troubled family. A typical urban poor family. My family's problems were quite simple. We were poor. No one from my immediate family managed to be rich. To expose others to riches. Our parents, well it never occurred to them to follow upon us. To educate and mould us into successful people. They could have done it. We were all very good in school. We needed a shepherd. My family had potential to produce a lawyer, doctor, professor, businesswoman, or an entrepreneur. We worked hard on our own. I was doing grade five in school. Time to commemorate the day of the children on the frontlines of war. In Angola a civil war was blazing. Many kids had lost leg and limb to land mines. To commemorate we were asked to do a poem on children on the frontlines. I went home played with my friends as usual. I was called for and ate dinner. I felt sleepy. It hit me, the assignment. I took pen and paper and began,

> 'Children on the frontline, running with babies on
>   their backs
> No food and clean drinking water, their clothes in rages
> Parents were raped and killed and young babies were
>   left and cries
> Children on the frontline, lets find guns and fight him'

The next day we passed our homework to the teacher. He sat at his desk and read quietly. He stood up and said 'there is one brilliant poem I want to read to the whole class.' he read it, making minor corrections as he did. The class was quiet as if they didn't understand. The teacher went on to show and read the poem to other teachers. A big relief from the other time I had developed cold feet in front of the school assembly. It was a proud moment!

There was the dark shadow of the threat of murder. The eighties were fearsome for me as a young kid. I became obsessed with fear of Gaigusi, Axe Killer and Richard Gwesela. These murderous characters used to haunt me a lot. They were remnants of the liberation war that had turned rogue. They didn't adjust to society. They were on a killing rampage. The murderous characters were a reminder of the lingering war in the southern region of my country. The conflict is still a contentious issue in my country. The best way to resolve it is compensation for the wrongs done. It was easier and cheaper if it had been done earlier. Any government that continue to ignore the issue is perpetuating a time bomb. Any hot head can bring it up at any opportune time in future. A tiny speck of fire burnt forests later. Clean up the mess before it becomes national filth.

As I grew up I noticed a lot of deficits in my life. They were pointed out by other kids mocking me while we were playing. We were going to school barefoot. In winter no jerseys until father brought home some jerseys made in awkward fashion. I had a hard time telling front from back. Everyone knew we didn't have a rural home. The only place we went for holidays was to my grandma Chihwiza's farm in a nearby town. My friends didn't consider the farm as rural enough. I became a wicked child. It must be around grade three. Father used to keep coins in new plastic pockets he got from his workplace. Those days coins were still valuable. There was the ½ cent coin but it was already on tits way out, 1 cent, 5 cents, up to 1 dollar coin. I started to pilfer father's coins. At first one five cent coin. I took more. I could see worry on my father's face. I think he was blaming it on mom. My dirty little habit grew until I was taking notes. I took one friend for a treaty and he was happy. He mentioned that he would tell his sister about my generosity. His sister was very close to my sister. I knew my game was in jeopardy. I didn't get caught and my sister never asked about it. I began to feel very guilty and I felt it. That what I was doing was wrong. I just stopped. From that day I never stole anything from the house or anywhere else. Today it's very hard for me to steal. The uneasiness alone will trade me off!

Poverty is a curse. When the ancestors give wounds the flies will eat you. Whenever a family is not stable thieves and perverts take advantage. They strike. My second sister doing form 2 was made pregnant by a man with three kids and a wife! My mom was completely unaware of what was happening. She thought that my sister had been bewitched and her stomach was swelling. She always relied on her mother for solutions. We made a journey to grandma to consult her. She confirmed that my sister was pregnant. Fortunately my sister turned out to be very strong. She resumed school up to degree level. She is a respected member of my community and a successful educator. She beat all odds.

During the eighties, the road that ran by my house was still gravel, dust and stones. Life was simple. A real buzz. The air of independence victory still fresh. Lots of expectations and some families were really ok. I remember married women playing ball in the gravel roads. Life was carefree. Certain characters in my society that time made life colourful. Some ex combatants came fresh from war. They stayed at home. They became restless they needed fun. One such ex combatant was Comrade as we popularly knew him. He used comrade instead of mister. He was my immediate neighbour. Our houses were very close separated only by a hedge. The effects of war were very evident on that family. There was a lot of energy at the house. Endless talking and endless fights. He regularly slaughtered a goat. There were endless traditional ceremonies. Comrade was full of war time antiques. He regularly dug holes fill them up with waste and top up with soil. Later it will be the family garden. He used skills he got from the war. He made his children sing the national anthem as punishment. Sometimes Comrade would go AWOL from his family. Days after he pitched up in a taxi with a young woman inside. He wore a white suit. He came to see the family then he disappears again. His daughter grew into a beautiful young girl. She was very naughty. One day she darted through the hedge to my house. She quickly pulled me inside my room. She sat on the bed and pulled me to her. She raised her dress. Full smooth thighs confronted me. She quickly opened and closed her thighs. She was impatient for action. I was hesitant, confused. I knew the danger. Her father's voice called. He was looking for her. She bolted out and ran to the front gate. She knew trouble when she heard his voice.

Comrade told me the secret of prison. 'Comrade why do you think they make people move about without underwear in prison? The essence, the strong smell of individual human is in the private parts. If you are not wearing underwear and you run away the dogs will easily sniff you out.' Learning truly never ends! He and his friend teamed up to beat one local girl accused of a political misdemeanour. They hit her with thin logs, prone position take. Same as they did in the war. They punished her. I heard my first gunshot in life when police opened fire on him. They arrested him. He liked to dress in shorts. He was as stealth as a cat. Most times police did not find him. He sneaked through my yard. Police were regular guests for him. He was in and out of jail. In the end he came out of jail sick. That sickness snuffed out his life.

We had one woman neighbour who was a prostitute. She rented one room with her three children, two girls and a boy. She used to bring her clients home. It's easier to condemn her but now I look and I see it differently. She was not noisy. She never fought and her clients were mature men who came discreetly. She managed to send all her children to school. When she realised that the trade had become dangerous because of AIDS and it generally didn't pay so much anymore, she started her own vegetable market stall. Whenever I met her in later years we always greeted and stop for a chat.

There was a certain breed of eccentric characters to be found around the neighbourhood. They tended to be grown up men and smart. They did not have money. They rented one room. They relied on being local heroes. One day one of the characters Charles, hired the service of a prostitute from the local club. It was late morning, around eleven when the fight broke out of the one room that Charles rented. It spilled into the street. The lady was still dressed in her night apparel. Big boots that reached her knees and a short mini skirt. She was curvy. I remember for quite some time in my young days ladies high boots gave me creeps. It later went away. They fought in the dusty road in broad daylight. We all gathered and witnessed Chale, as we affectionately called him, twist her hair and kick her until she fell into the dust. The long hair becoming blonde from the red soil. People stopped the fight. The lady reported to police. Chale had not paid for services. The picture remained in my memory. It was common to hear one of the young boys in the neighbourhood shouting, 'my name is Chale! I will hit you!' We sometimes played hide and seeks. It involved a ball. The one who got hit by the ball had to find someone to hit with the ball and so on. We went through the alleys and in between houses playing that game. Those days there were no walls or fences surrounding houses. In one of the game I passed through Chale's rented house. He was standing outside talking to Girly the landlord's beautiful daughter. I was young but I was sure I saw an urgent bulge pushing in front of Chale's trousers. I bumped into them another day. The same bulge was persistent. I forgot about it. A year later Girly was pregnant with Chale's baby. He didn't marry her.

The other peculiar guy was Jesus. He didn't drink alcohol or smoke. We called him Jesus because he was tall and handsome. He kept a long beard. He jogged daily at sunset. He was strong and handsome. He did not have money. He rented one room. He went on to take one of the most beautiful girls around that time. Her father was bitter. He had hoped she would do better.

The other cranky characters were the three brothers who stayed with us. They rented one room. The eldest was a qualified air force pilot. He was discharged due to mental illness. He was intelligent. He was into fucking ladies. He brought one lady ambassador from a neighbouring country, Botswana to his room. He came out and told me and my brother to watch from the window. He had left the curtain slightly open. We enjoyed watching him as he screwed the woman for quite a long time. Mosquitoes made us to go inside. He was still at it. Sometimes he liked to catch houseflies with his bare hands. He showed me each one he killed. He killed quite a lot. By the time he finished I was feeling nauseous. He introduced me to the English dictionary for the first time. 'Even orange is in there?' I asked. He opened the page and showed me 'orange' in the dictionary! I knew the dictionary is the silo of all words. He's the one who took me into town for the first time. We used the local bus written DAF in front, inherited from the previous regime. It was quite special to board a bus. The smell of diesel and the power of the engine as the bus growled on into the city, unforgettable. He took me and my brother around famous spots but he left us alone way up in Fifth Street. We asked our way back home. The smell of the city remained to sweeten the deal. He ticked his calendar on days he fucked ladies. He made one of the local girls pregnant but didn't marry her.

His younger brother cooked soap the whole day. Those were the days his turn of the psychiatric circle was on. Another brother used to spot permed hair. He wore pointed shoes. It was exciting when he came back from college. His friends would visit. He's the one who showed me my first sight of an STD infection. He brought home one light skinned girl from town. The next week he started limping. I asked him what was wrong. He opened his trousers. What a ghastly big blob, grey and quivery on his groin. He was in pain. One night this brother's circle of psychiatry became fearsome. We slept in the lounge. It was after 1 am. The brother got into an altercation with drunkards. They didn't know he was ill. They beat him with bamboo ropes. He ran straight home, tried to enter but the front door was locked. He attacked the upper part made of glass with his bare hands. The glass gave way. He reached inside opened and entered. God was looking after us.

I experienced an unease moment. I bought a t shirt in town from the Indian shops. The Indian merchants were very naughty. They printed t shirts written, 'we are living very well, we only witness poverty in our neighbour's house.' Written in indigenous language it sounded funny. I fell for it and bought one. At home I wore it once. I couldn't face my neighbours. I never wore it again! There were families that had influence. One such family stayed a few lines form our house. The mother of that family was very active in community projects. She used to wear a brown uniform and with other ladies in that committee they used to inspect households for cleanliness. I admired her. Her family was doing quite well. Her children had good jobs. Later as the economy bite, the husband sold the house to my uncle who was a soldier. He did it secretly and relocated to the village. He married another woman and settled there. The wife in town was surprised when she was told to vacate. She resisted until my uncle passed away. His son got lawyers' help and he kicked her out. There was a girl lived behind my house. She fell in love with one notorious womaniser who was married. They didn't have anywhere to go for a frolic. They opted to go into the hill which was nearby. She stepped on human shit. When she came down the hill, the whole way she took was smelly. That hill was popular with couples in the eighties. My cousin used it with one prostitute he took from the council bar. He forgot his underwear. He went to look for it the next day and found it! My elder brother used to laugh about it as he told me the story.

Godmother was always an avid reader. One afternoon I sat with her in the lounge. She was doing her homework. I was watching TV. One of the books she put on the table attracted my attention. It was poetry and the title was hard to read. I asked godmother how to spell the word. She reprimanded. 'Search any words you don't know from the dictionary.' 'I wouldn't understand the explanation' I put in. In the end she told me the dictionary meaning. 'Reverberation is the resound in a succession of echoes. To have a prolonged or continuing effect. In life when we do good deeds, they reverberate throughout generations to come.' Godmother patiently explained. The war was over but vigilantism was rife. It felt weird when I passed by houses with windows broken. Fear was my companion. Party clashes continued after independence. We used to live in perpetual fear. Party youth meetings meant forced attendance. Boys in the neighbourhood eagerly participated. The meetings gave them a chance to engage with girls. They gave pressure for all able bodied young persons to attend. The meetings were held around six at night. Godmother hated the meetings. She was concerned about her school work. She hid from the door to door gangs that hunted all young people. One guy who stayed in front of our house became the chairperson. He gave Godmother a hard time. Later that guy was tempted by the sweet lure of money. He was lucky to get a job in the city. He stole money from his company. He used it to hire taxis, marry a light skinned woman and generally squander the ill gotten money. He got caught and did time.

Politicians can make wrong decisions that may affect lives forever. Sometimes even destroy dreams. Rarely do politicians get it right and implement programmes that benefit people. Most decisions they make are based on political relevance. The government of my country implemented economic structural adjustment programme or ESAP. It almost destroyed my dreams to zero. My education was threatened. My father got redundant from work. Soon after independence the government got support from foreign donors to mend the economy. The programme seemed to have worked. For a short period we had a credible economy.

By the 1990s government abolished wage controls. It limited government expenditure and devalued the local currency by 40 per cent. They ceased subsidies on consumer goods. Government also opened up the foreign currency allocation system. They got rid of protection of non-productive import substituting industries.

Government increased profit remittance abroad. It drastically restructured government owned corporations and other public enterprises. The majority of people became poorer. People were caught unaware of the real hard grind of the programme. The government advertised that it would transform lives. I learnt never to trust politicians. My experience of politicians exposing people to danger is still ongoing. Each day brings new scandals that expose huge problems in politicians' credibility. Companies retrenched workers en masse. They gave packages meant for workers to start their own business. Everyone felt the bite of a poor economy.

War veterans of the war of liberation began to show agitation. Poverty literary spiralled. Local dailies were reporting that current poverty assessments showed over 70 % of us people were wallowing in abject poverty. The newspapers were talking about what they termed 'food poverty line' which they put at over 50 %. Hunger made people do evil like kill for little money. Walking at night became dangerous. Father was working in the local council bar. It was quite a distance away from the house. He walked because his bicycle had been stolen. The road he took passed through a park. Night shift he finished at midnight and walked alone to the house. This was treacherous. I was in form two in school. My brother was in form three. We went to the council bar at 1130 pm every night my father was doing night shift. It was winter. Passing through my school friend's house, all lights out and I imagined him enjoying warm blankets. There was a big guy who stayed along the road we used. He was rumoured to be one of the muggers. Every time he stared at us and never said anything. One day he approached father. He told him that there was no protection because we were so young. Any one could rob him with or without us. It was a scary encounter.

We said bye to scary encounters. Economic reforms made my father redundant. He was given a small package to start his own business. He tried to sell fruits and veggie. His only skill was in bar tending. He bought a cart which he pushed around the suburb. He often stood by the street which I used with my friends coming from school. It was a real heart wrenching time for me. My friends all became quiet as we passed by my father and his cart. Somehow his fruits and veggie were dying out. The mangoes overripe with black splotches. He did not have the experienced eye to pick out fresh fruit that would last longer. He was looking haggard. Before, he was selling in one place the bar, now he pulled a cart around the area. He suffered high blood pressure. I had my eye on one beautiful girl staying near my house. We usually went home together from school. She always bought an orange or apple from my father. She was kind.

Ice Cube, starring in 'Friday' was my hero and role model. The man just exuded coolness. Cool as an ice cube! I knew that real life was not Ice Cube and smoking weed but it helped to lull down the pain of everyday misery. I had been smoking weed for a while. I always had small money. I was running a backyard barber shop. I tried to sell weed on the side but stopped. I was too scared to get caught. I stuck to smoking it and doing hair. I would have been better off if I had not tasted weed. It was hard to escape the scourge. Weed is strictly illegal in my country as well as everywhere except Amsterdam and in the US legislation to legalise is under way. In my country, it was easily available because a lot of people smoked.

One day a friend three houses away came and quietly took me to his room at his house. He locked the door and lighted a joint. He smoked it and passed to me. It was easy for me to smoke it. I had experimented with cigarette smoking before. I puffed and passed it back. I took it dragged it second time and I thought that it was not effective. I didn't feel anything. I kept dragging until I coughed. I passed it to my friend. It suddenly hit me. A sharp sensation shot down to the foot. The middle of the head felt like a great hand was clamping it. It felt very euphoric and light. I floated the rest of that day. I was in dreamland. My mouth felt very dry. I enjoyed this first experience enough to try it again. And again. The initiator later had psychiatric problems. He jumped and sang in the street at midnight. He was sent to hospital and stayed one week. When he came back he was quite normal. He had gained weight and was on medication. He made it a habit to visit the barber shop and he found us puffing away. He warned 'oh I see you are still smoking. Soon we will be going to the psychiatry unit to see one of you there.' It used to scare us. My cousin stopped smoking weed.

One other friend erupted two weeks after the initiator's one. He really went haywire. I was told by his neighbour that he had been kicking dishes at home the previous night. He warned that we should not give him weed. The next day we were puffing as usual. The guy burst inside the barbershop intoxicated by psychiatric energy. He was holding two bricks. God intervened. He went away without attacking anyone. He later took off his dangalee jeans in the street. He wasn't wearing underwear. It was quite a spectacle. Sometimes weed has the tendency to make you say out what you are thinking but do not necessarily want the other person to hear. My friend's brother had been ill for a long time. One day my friend came to tell me his brother had succumbed. Unfortunately he came just after I had smoked a joint. I was thinking the brother had rested. I proceeded to shake his hand in accordance with local tradition. I said 'congratulations.' He looked at me confused. I quickly realised my error. I said sorry. That is the dark side of weed.

What really drew me to Ice was the coolness. The courage when he fought Deebo, the evil giant. The mood was captured right. It became contagious when Cube's father, the old man who was first introduced taking a shit in the bathroom, making everyone late, started mimicking the fight in celebration to Ice's victory. Oh, that movie really did set me off. Although it was hilariously funny, it also showed the desperate lives young black man were facing. The house breaks, selling weed, Deebo the neighbourhood bully taking advantage of people already on the edge. The reality of it touched a nerve in me. In my back yard barber shop I made improvements. I put up a proper precast wall, a decent roof and painted the inside. I hung mirrors and connected fluorescent lights. It was cool. I also bought one car seat for people to sit while waiting to have a cut.

Sometimes in the afternoon it became quiet. Bored girls in my hood came and sat on that seat and we chat.

The mind of an adolescent is amazing. I used to enjoy so much these visits because the seat was meant for a car, so it was so low, when you sit you have to raise your legs. Most girls would be cautious at first and kept their legs shut. As conversation intensified they relaxed. It was perfect view for me. That was the fun part, but I was seriously making enough to buy food in the house and still have some to spend. I realised at an early age the importance of keeping my head up, even in difficult circumstances. Reality was never too far from me to snooze. The economic situation was hard. I was subsidising my own education! The government cut back on subsidies. Bread and salt became expensive. For my family with meagre income from my father it was very tough.

In later adolescents we started experimenting sexually. An exciting adventure of forbidden pleasure. With the danger of unwanted pregnancy and disease lurking. My first sexual encounter was very sweet but the girl had a very smelly pussy. She was beautiful. She had one kid given to her by the notorious womaniser who took the girl behind my house to the hill where she stepped on shit. I thought I loved her. On the first encounter I did it facing her. After a long while she pushed me aside. She went on all fours with her buttocks open. Inexperience took over. I was taken aback. In the end we had to resume missionary. That illicit fornication went on until one day I felt itchiness in my penis. I asked one guy who was senior in fucking ladies. He told me that itchiness with heat when passing urine meant infection. He advised me to see a doctor. I was shy. My body started to feel feverish. I thought about one older guy in my hood who suffered from untreated infection. In the end I hit my heart to stone. I went to the doctor who practiced nearby at the shopping lot. He told me it was gonorrhoea. He gave me an injection and said I should bring my partner. He further sent me for tests to confirm his diagnosis and also an HIV test. I couldn't eat well for 3 days waiting for the dreaded result. Lucky it came positive for gonorrhoea and not HIV. From that day I never slept with that girl again. Since that time it became hard for me to be promiscuous. The first cut is the deepest.

My older friend who suffered trusted one short stocky man for a doctor. The man was from neighbouring Malawi. Most from there are attributed with Prowse in healing and killing herbs. So he told the man his problem. The short man said that it was very easy. My friend was given a big bottle full of reddish herbs immersed in water. He was instructed to drink it until it finished. He took 2 days gulping the bitter herbs. He went back and told the man nothing had improved, actually he was worse. The man asked to see. The guy shifted his trouser down. The whiff of bad meat was strong immediately. The short stocky man looking pensive whispered 'I think you should try the clinic.' That advice healed the guy.

I met my fair share of loose girls in the suburb. One girl who stayed in my hood changed character dramatically. She went to a good school in town. She was quiet and reserved. She completed school and stayed home. She was hit upon by the notorious womaniser who was married. Her relationship with him was short. It left her scarred. She became wanton. The girl was very easy to sex with. Boys flocked to her like flies to an infected wound. One naughty boy staying near my place became her boyfriend. He took her to his house and fucked her. He got bored and called me and two other friends. The guy left the light off. He gave his t shirt to the friend. The friend went inside and fucked the girl. The second guy got the same t shirt and fucked her. I got the t shirt and went in. I approached the girl. She lay with her head covered by a blanket. Her voluptuous thighs were bared. I went nearer. She groped for me in the dark. She caressed my chest. She moved her hand up to my head and screamed. Her boyfriend had full hair in his head. I was bald as a baby's bum.

Strange things happened in the suburb. One woman who had settled down well with one guy living near my house made a stunning transformation after the guy's demise. They had two children already and the guy got sick and passed on. She remained at the house but slowly started visiting the local club and council bar. It was very embarrassing but she was okay with it. Another guy staying in front of my house became naughty right from his first pay check. His family background was strict. His brother was the one who reported me at home when he caught me smoking with the brother of the initiator. On one of his escapades he took me along. We first went to the local shopping centre to wait for his partner. He bought two cokes and we sipped. Later she came and we walked to the local disused market building and there he fucked her standing. I was very near. I could hear the girl sing and the cluck of wet impact. He did the same two or more times I am not sure. Other times I was not there. After two weeks I saw him riding his bike with his legs opened awkwardly. I asked him why the awkward style. He told me, 'I've been bitten' he was infected, STD. The promiscuity was at all level of society. Throw HIV, a disease transmitted sexually into play. People were caught unaware. A huge number of people perished. This guy was lucky he remained free of the virus and disease. Each and every deceased is accorded a funeral typical of all urban people despite their status. A three or two day vigil with people from all walks coming in to pay last respects. The homeless of course will take advantage of the free food, some company, and warm fire. Most dearly to their vagrant hearts, free booze! This is how my people look after each other. Every one gets a decent burial. How gracious it would be for my people to work and attain a decent livelihood for everyone.

Sheer determination saw my elder sister pass her o levels. She applied for office work. She was invited by one company and I went with her to look for the place before she went for the interview. It was in the affluent area of the city near the reserve bank building. I looked at the high stories. I couldn't believe she would work there one day. She went for the interview but she was not clear if she got it or not. They had informed her of her working hours and terms of employment. I told her 'you got the job!' We hugged and celebrated just the two of us. Mom had run away again that time.

High school blues. In all my life I will never forget that slap. I was late for geography class. The teacher called me. I never suspected he would slap me. I was ready with an explanation. I leaned toward him. Lighter! A double clap that left my head exploding. I went and sat down. I was dazed. I couldn't look anyone in the eyes. The teacher was local but studied in Australia. He pronounced his words with an accent foreign to us. He was smart fashion wise. When he talked he hung his fingers down like ladies do. A new skinny lady teacher came to my school. My geography teacher quickly coupled with her. They hit it off. My geography teacher began to look poor. His hair became brown, his face dull. He did not change clothes as often as before. He became thin. He transferred to another school. I never saw him again. Good riddance.

Before I completed my 'A' levels a tragedy happened. It introduced me to the elusive nature of life. I felt one very strong emotion when it happened. Fear. He was my friend from the lower level. He didn't continue to 'A' level. He got a job in the tobacco industry. It was a good job that gave him six months off the job but getting paid every month. My friend was handsome and intelligent. We spent almost every day of life together. One day as he disembarked from the bus in front of his workplace, a car coming from the blind side hit him. He flew into the air whilst his shoe flew inside the durawall of his workplace! He was taken to hospital. He passed on before I could see him. I went to his burial. He was my only friend. Life changed forever for me. It was no longer as I had visualised it in lower secondary school.

I was the recipient of the economics best student in all form six pupils. I was surprised. Languages were my strong points! I was asked to prepare a presentation for that day. I felt like I needed the toilet. Memories of long ago came when I got stuck in front of an assembly of pupils flooded back. I went home and cracked my head. At last I took pen and paper and wrote lines down. I looked at them. They were simple lines saying how I felt at that particular time.

Don't throw it away

Attention my little one
Cock your ears well
To my humble words
Honed by experience of life
Be careful of the company you keep
For if you hang out with bums
And you don't bum yourself
I will blow a trumpet in your honour

When others your age take the syringe
Full of illicit drugs that destroy
Take your pen
Full of ink that bring forth wisdom

Life is short
Don't make it shorter
By smoking and alcohol abuse
Exercise, study and give meaning to life

Remember we are our own enemy
So listen well, avoid self destruction
Appreciate your family
And stand by it, protect and love it

Promise to never be a regular inmate
At the local jailhouse
Crime is your enemy
And only good deeds will give you a future

Take my wise counsel
And you triumph

Throw it away
And you throw away life!

I completed my advanced level. I loafed around for six months before I got an office job. This was not due to favourable employment chances. Godmother had it all figured. She recommended me to the bosses of a certain company. Unemployment was a pain and an exodus of young skilled professionals had been in progress. A lot of people were going to Botswana, South Africa, Britain, US, Canada, Australia and some New Zealand. The fact that my country faced a rapidly increasing unemployment crisis is evident in the percentage drop of the total population of the formally employed. It dropped drastically. The problem of unemployment continued to worsen. I started off as a filing clerk and rose through the ranks to client's services team leader. I rose no more.

CHAPTER 3

As we entered into the 90s the Zimbabwean dollar was devalued repeatedly. A crisis that started with the land redistribution process rendered the local currency valueless. The official rate of 55 local dollars to 1 US dollar that government was using was not true. It created an unofficial black market rate of 300 local dollars to 1 US dollar. When the economy was liberalised a lot of cheap imported goods from South Africa flooded the market. Agriculture was hugely reduced by a drought. As a result many men found themselves unemployed. The newspapers were also reporting that South Africa had enacted a tariff on my country's textile exports. So industries were affected. I experienced the pain of existing in a country with a GDP that plummeted minus eleven per cent from 1991 to early 2000s. The danger of existing in such a harsh environment is real. The systematic targeting of voices of descent becomes more rampant as government tries to stifle any uprisings. In my country intimidation to freedom to information continues even today and since I grew up in that society I always resent authority.

When independence came Thomas Mapfumo continued his revolution style. He sang about current issues affecting the people. He sang about murder in politics, corruption in the society and failure of the current government. He reminded the government that it thought ploughing was easy. 'Maiti kurima inyore' directly translated into my country's dialect. This was brilliant art in its most potent form. It was at odds with the government. They were upon him. He ran away into exile in the United States of America. He had stepped out.

Meanwhile in 1997 the war veterans demanded pensions and gratuities from the government. The funds were paid unbudgeted for. The economy went into a free fall. People who were managing before could not because of foreign currency shortages. Ordinary people like me were affected instantly by the government's economic disaster. Political tensions resulted in the formation of a new party. It almost toppled the government in later years. Government reintroduced price controls. This resulted in the proliferation of the black market. There was a time when we bought everything on the black market.

How does a revolutionary explain the forgiveness of his agriculture minister who sold the strategic grain reserve of the country? As fate would have it, there was a drought the very next year. The revolutionary leader authorised the government to buy grain from the country that thieving minister had sold grain to. We were all afraid to step out and say 'enough!' I'm afraid to step out. The police in my country are masters of punishment beatings. They give a beating popularly known as, 'die later.' Later as the country slide into internal struggles against Bob's wish in his song 'Zimbabwe', there were notable characters that stood out. They challenged the status quo. They were immediately silenced. They became alienated form the people. One man uneducated to the level of the perfect revolutionary stepped out. It takes the courage to step out. Tsvangirai of the opposition did it. I respect and note him for stepping out. Politics cannot fully explain the significance of the fact that he did step out. He challenged the status quo. Individual sacrifice rather than politics is needed in order to step out. To me he remains relevant. He suffered for it. Was brutally assaulted physically. They could not douse a fire that was already burning. 'It's a fire!' sang Bob Marley in his song 'Ride natty ride'.

The tragedy of my life repeated itself. Mom had run away to her mother at Chihwiza farm. The reason was she had a dispute with the old man, our father. My sister broke the news to me. I felt rage. I asked her why everyone just let mom go. They were all there. My sister told me it had happened so fast. I knew my sister was the strongest in character. She would have stopped mom if she had the chance. I was to blame. I had chosen to stay away thinking it was one of the usual fights. I was dead wrong. Our family house had no mom. It certainly was a circle. My father became a bachelor for a while. He was a former bar man, the 'girls' he saw were the women who went to the bar. Each time mom ran away, a local known prostitute would take the reigns of mom. It was devastating. Amazingly if mom came back he would receive her. Life would quickly turn to normal in the house. Deep scars invisible to the eye would be left. We boarded a public taxi to my sister's house. 'Changes' by Tupac was blasting at high volume, as is the trend with the public transport drivers. The words captured me. I looked at my sister. She bit her lips suppressing the urge to cry. I could see the tears glistening in her eyes as she looked back at me. The pain was there. She always took much of the pain. She had grown up naturally responsible. She used to play mommy when mom ran away.

The bleary days never ended. Political misdirection was making it tough. Zimbabwe is South Africa's largest trading partner on the continent. The country largely exports primary goods to South Africa. It is dependant on South Africa for fuel and electricity. The trading balance is in favour of South African exports of mainly manufactured products to Zimbabwe. South Africa's trade practices resulted in Zimbabwe's goods being less competitive in South Africa and this has affected my country's economy. The land question became a political tool. The law as we knew it before had changed. Rowdy youths assembled and set up permanent base in nearby bushes. They stationed at the local shopping centre in the name of the ruling party. They beat up people at the slightest altercation with them.

The biggest disease of the human species is playing the selfish drum continuously. My eldest cousin took my eldest brother for drinking rides in his car. He poisoned him during these escapades. Before we knew it my brother was talking like him. I used to wonder why our brother seemed so out of focus with reality. My family was vulnerable and alienated. It needed a son to protect it. The cousin led my brother to focus on abstract extended family issues. The cousin was the leader of interrogations. His brothers and sisters were his lieutenants. They bombarded me and my closest brother on why we never visited relatives? Why we don't know people? Who is this? One cousin fished out of his pocket coins. He commanded us to visit them next weekend. It was a drunken circus. No one ever saw how sensitive we were. The more they shouted the more we withdrew. They tried to force us into what should have been all along. You can take a horse to the river but I bet you can never force it to drink. They were all older than us. They knew the problems mom had with her mother in law. They knew how we came to be alienated. They weren't being honest.

Whenever there was a social gathering, say a funeral, elder cousin overshadowed everyone. He made all the arrangements. He gave the big speech in which he lets everyone know the big fish. He reminded all that at another funeral he prevented another relative from facing a pauper burial. All relatives were aware of him. People developed paralysis if he was not there. He ran amok with his ego. He quarrelled with everyone. He did strange things, taboos to culture like playing music at a funeral. Elderly people have a way of referring behaviour they do not understand to traditional terms. To them anything that smells of evil will be attributed to witchcraft. They knew that the cousin challenges and belittles every one around. They wondered how come so much power and belligerence? He is a male witch! They concluded. Word started being whispered around. Soon it started to resemble truth. It affected even sceptics like me who do not normally believe in witchcraft. I become unsure of my beliefs. Who the cap fits let them wear it. It doesn't make the situation better for me when I overheard him talking on his phone. He spoke in derogatory terms about my recently dead brother. Only a devil would do that. Add insult to injury. At yet another family gathering, the elder cousin was fuming and ranting that people were accusing him of witchcraft. He claimed that he got his money through hard work. I told him yes people were actually saying he was a male witch. He replied that next time I heard anyone say that I should immediately inform him. He will confront the person.

The elder cousin spent a lot of energy on futile activities. Ceaseless intake of alcohol, a sharp tongue and a malicious mind. He was in a good position to make an everlasting positive impact on me. He chose to bully me into submission. He drove me to feel that something was wrong with me and my family. He could have left us alone. He wouldn't have lost anything. I would respect him as my rarely seen relative. He chose to torment innocent children who needed help. Our other cousin who worked at the local council was a decent respectful man. I used to hear about him. One day I went to the council to pay bills. He was on duty. He did not know me. He saw the name on the card. He told me to stand aside and wait for him. I was confused but I did as he said. After he cleared the people he came and told me in polite terms that he was my cousin. He explained that his mother and my father were blood brother and sister. He emphasised again that we were relatives. Of course it sounded remote. We had never met. As I grew up and I met him more often I always knew and respected him. He drinks beer at gatherings but he never become reckless with speech. The other brother who everyone says is a thief and a bum is a much better person to me. He was never rude to me. The tree that got cut always bears the scars and the mischievous axe soon forgets.

I experienced the turmoil and struggles of a ruling elite threatened by a strong opposition. All along there was no genuine opposition to refer to. The once weak and meek opposition movement had resurged into a formidable peoplepower. History was being rolled out. Times were changing! Much of the information on what was affecting us I got from the daily news. It was safe to read in the capital city only. Beyond the capital, holding a copy of the daily news invited a thorough beating by the militias. The Daily News printing press was located adjacent to my suburb. Around 3 am I woke up. The deep bang was extraordinary. It sounded like a bomb. The next morning I heard on the local radio station that the daily news press was bombed. The perpetrators were never found.

The Danse Macabre collects people from all walks of life. I read about one colonialist in my history book in school. His name was Cecil John Rhodes. They were sleeping in a tent. Suddenly he awoke his companion, Starr Jameson. Jameson was alarmed thinking that maybe the tent was on fire. He was surprised when Cecil said to him 'have you ever thought how lucky we are to be born British, the finest flower of civilisation?' Lucky or not he faced demise. That is what equals everyone. It was three in the early morning. My hand phone rang. I started, rubbed my eyes and grabbed the phone. I said 'hallo.' Godmother was on the line. From her voice I knew it had happened. She didn't say anything. She held on the line. I could hear the storm of grieving heavy in the air . . . The first time I came face to face with Death in the family was earlier. The second born in my family died after falling sick. This time it came with a vengeance. The eldest son of the family was gone. Godmother had tried her best but the dance was on. I felt for Godmother. She had lost her only son earlier. The pain was still fresh. She was facing yet more mourning. Ashes to ashes dust to dust. We held the funeral. At the funeral my cousin played music, a taboo in my culture. I confronted him about it. I told him to stay away and not agitate mourners. He was aggressive.

Soon after the funeral for my brother Godmother left me. She went overseas to further her studies. I was left alone and vulnerable. I'd always relied on Godmother. I was in debt amounting over half my salary. Pay day came. I paid back all debts. I was left with enough change for a few beers and a cheese roll. The next day I went to my colleagues asking for a loan. That time my country was going into a melt down. It never stopped. It was one crisis after another. Prices in supermarkets were being changed twice a day. The governor of the central bank printed more money. He ran out of new currency figures. He resorted to issuing bearer checks. There was a cash squeeze on the public. It became a daily battle right at the beginning of the day. Everyone would be out looking for transport to take them to work. The government was in a dispute with western nations. It was slapped with economic sanctions. Sanctions meant no fuel and public transport. We fought for the few public cars available. A lot of drama happened. Some jumped over people's heads. A packed greasy lunch box burst open and mess everyone nearby. The bus terminus witnessed a lot of fist fights. People settled instant disagreements like jumping the queue.

I usually arrived at work dishevelled. That time I kept a nice English cut. My hair would be a mess. I went to the men's room first. I wiped my dusty shoes, my trousers and comb my hair. I entered the office more presentable. Tea break was a cup of tea we got free from the canteen. I went downstairs to buy one stick of cigarette. I feel real hunger gnawing me. Its lunch break. I have no money to buy lunch. At the end of the day more hardship awaited. I see throngs of people all hoping to catch a ride home. It's apparent there is no transport. Some ladies and gentlemen gave bribes to the rank marshals to get first preference when the bus came. For us who had not paid we had to battle it out until we made it inside. Inside the bus we are packed. The decent space limitation between men and women is grossly violated. Many a time a woman would scream out after feeling rigid poking from the poor male tightly packed into her. In countries with decent economies this is considered gross violation of public decency. Here it was daily. With hunger gnawing again I was happy to reach home. Warm food prepared by my girlfriend was waiting. A man could grow white hair and take pension facing the same routine. Mom was still at the farm and father was a bachelor.

I took my old Mazda 323 1982 model, left to me by Godmother, from the garage. It had been repaired. I went to see father at the house. It was dark around the house. I knocked father came and opened for me. He was sleeping already. We went to his bedroom. He gave me a chair and I sat down. He sat on the bed. We talked for quite a while. As I was about to announce my departure I looked down. I went, 'oh! What happened to your legs!?' they were swollen. He took it easy. I was alarmed. He was sick. The next day I visited again. I took him to a specialist doctor. He told me father was very sick. He should have sought treatment earlier. Three months later he passed on. My life dropped further down to gloom kingdom come. Death is dark and weird. It took father away before I could prove myself to him. Pamper him like any proud son would want to do. He passed on when we had begun to communicate like adults. With mutual respect. I felt closer to him. I showed him I was not going to judge him about the women he brought home. Our relationship was above that. I hoped for more time to spoil and dote on him. Maybe that one time we could make it right. Have peace and love in the family.

The following year my closest brother became sick. Mom had come back home. A lot of things still needed to be done. I took my ill brother to stay with me. I struggled with my closest brother's illness. We looked after him as best as we could. Sometimes we sent him to hospital, bring him home the next day and the third day send him to hospital again. It was hard. One particular night there were political riots. I sacrificed to take him to hospital. Ambulances were not available, overwhelmed by demand. On my way back I bumped into a group of youths who blocked the road with stone boulders. I crushed into them. They pulled me out of the car and shook me up. They took all my valuables. Lucky they didn't outright beat me up.

The most heart rending situation was that Godmother was facing death in hospital. She was alone battling for her life. The doctors later told her that at one moment they thought they would lose her. No relative was with her except her only close friend. I needed to talk to my sister. She had always been there to provide practical solutions. As my brother's life ebbed away she revived. On the last day of his life I managed to call her at the hospital. I told her brother had gone.

I cried and cried. I knew she was still frail so I tried and eventually stifled the crying. Godmother was still in hospital. That was a dark time in life. Godmother resolved not to go easily. She defeated and cut the pattern that was reducing us. She said enough was enough. The Danse macabre had run its full course. My family was cut in half, from eight members to four members. Godmother told me, 'Mbiramatako, we don't know much about life, or where to hide from hardship and death. We don't know who can help us. We only have ourselves to rely on. We have to move on. Make sure whenever you can to say this simple prayer,

Our father who art in heaven, hallowed is thy name
Thy kingdom come, thy will be done on earth as in
    heaven
Give us this day our daily bread, forgive us our sins
As we forgive those who trespass against us
Give us our daily bread, and lead us not into
    temptation
But deliver us from evil
Forever and ever
Amen

A month after my brother's funeral, I came back from work. My girlfriend was not around but was nearby. I went into the bathroom to take a pee. Something struck me, the picture of my frail brother passing urine while I waited and watched over him. The strong pang of pain was real, constricting my insides so that I began to breath fast. I tried to control the wave. I knew my girlfriend would be back any minute. I didn't want her to see me crying. The emotion was too strong. Without warning I wept like a small boy, 'my brother?' I wailed. Strong sobs of grief I didn't show during the burial rites for him. I heard the front door open. I quickly composed myself, washed my face and joined my girlfriend in the lounge. She asked me what was wrong. I told her it was ok. She went to the kitchen and began preparing dinner. I sat down to watch TV. My friend came and suggested to go out for a beer nearby. I told my girl but she didn't reply. She was angry already. I was at the door. She shouted that dinner was ready. I replied that I would eat later. At the same time I closed the door. I went to the car without looking back. My friend was driving. He had one girl in front. In the back where I sat there was another girl, young like her friend in front. Along the way to the bar we got acquainted. By the time we reached the bar we were chatting like good old friends.

The bar was fashioned to be a beer garden with barbeque and drinks. We sat outside and ordered a round of beers. Whilst waiting for the drinks we ordered some beef barbeque and salad. We continued with conversation. I took a close look at the girl for the first time. She was beautiful. The way the seats were arranged made us sit very close. She was wearing a tiny denim mini skirt. It left a generous amount of her thighs to my view. The legs were smooth and long. I felt my member start to receive more blood. Our drinks arrived. We sipped and things became real cosy. The barbeque came we paid. We imbibed and took bites of succulent fresh barbeque beef and fresh salad. By the end of our outing we were all gay and happy. On the way home the girl became erotically restless. I felt a keen electric flash. It stirred my member to full attention. Instantly she noticed the bulge. She rubbed lightly over it with her soft hand. I caught my breath. At that moment my friend was asking me if I wanted to go home. Or first go to his bachelor flat. I quickly told him to proceed to his flat. Once we reached my friend grabbed two beers from the fridge. He shouted that there was more and he shut his bedroom door. The girl didn't give me a chance to take the beers. She was upon me kissing and rubbing her body against my lean hard form. She went down on her knees. I bent down and lightly ran my hand on the mound of pussy covered by small flimsy panties. She caught her breath. I am well endowed down there. She could never miss it. But my dick was limp. She tried to lick it. In the end I had to apologise. I went to the bathroom. I looked at my face in the mirror.

My eyes were vacant. God, I was a wreck. I was still in mourning. Sexual pleasure could not appease the emptiness. Almost everyone who was close to me was gone. I felt a dead weight. I needed to own up and pay my respects,

Requiem

I appreciate indubitable men in dash
To all folk I celebrated trice solely
Callow and sophisticated in spirit
I assumed it nevermore pass,
That we would be detached lone hour
You abscond incognito, me ad hoc in obscurity
Dimension abide
Are you with the pervading breeze that enshroud us?
Do you gape at me? Please ante up a hint
You light out antecedent, I am dubious
Adlib, unbidden or the call of moirai
You split.

Accredited philosophy, you are there ultimately
I fathom not the savoir faire of turf you dwell
I only await angst of death
The only form to purview you, or is else plot?
Forasmuch as I avowed confidentially but now departed
One of you shine me just a small sign
I yearn to acquaint the other side beyond repose
Perchance we will reconcile in else realm
I anguish faux pas
Visions nevermore executed in this realm.
You all exited fresh,
The utmost detritus I apperceive bona fide anima.

CHAPTER 4

Hardship made me more spiritual and philosophical. After tragedy after tragedy the family agreed that evil spirits gave us a hard time. They agreed the solution lay in faith healing and religion. I begged to differ. I could not oppose them directly. That did not stop me from thinking. The little money my family had was wasted on paying for faith healing services and tithes. It astonished me that we relied on prophets. New churches boast of new members. Either straight from home or from another church. The people who change churches should ask themselves who was looking after them in the transition period? It seemed easier to resort to miracles. Believe for example, that weight of the obese can be reduced in real time by the wonders of a prophet. Some of my family members believed this. I believed logic prevails in the spiritual as well as physical realm. I had nothing against the prophets. The governor of the county exonerated them of any wrong doing. My concern was the ignorance that people exhibited. The blind never questioning faith.

I observed one pastor's approach to gospel. He told people directly that he was going to take their money. That they had made an agreement with God. He was only the receiver. He told the congregation that they gave money not because he asked them to, but because he had just convinced them that what he preached to them was God speaking. He is quite intelligent. It is indeed miracle money when a young pastor preach. People voluntarily stand up and put money right there. Before the official tithes giving time. The ushers swept it with brooms to keep it together. If the recipient is thrifty and good with money, they can become instant millionaires using that money. There is no stealing. Religion is a choice that we make individually and will defend fiercely ourselves. This young pastor happens to have an accounting degree. The young man said that Christianity started in Israel and the Romans made it a religion, the British made it a culture, Americans made it business and Africa made it spirituality. Wake up Africans he urges. So how does he take Christianity himself? I am not sure. My view is that religion is a social gathering that influences order and behaviour in society. It is desirable when used honestly. When it is used to hoodwink innocent and ill people, it becomes bad religion right there. I know that, subtle is the Lord, not malicious.

We should know not believe. One famous scientist said that human knowledge using science has been limited, has hit the wall. Everyday, discoveries are being made which continue to push the wall further. We could discover some things which we never imagined in our present lives. A lot of strong convictions will be left exposed positively or negatively. Negative exposure if the belief is proved wrong. Galileo discovered the telescope and consequently he discovered that the world was round not flat. The planets actually circle around the sun and not that everything circles around the earth. The church made a stance that the earth was flat and everything circled around the earth. As a result of Galileo's discovery, the church was left exposed.

I watched a documentary called 'What would you do?' That documentary is powerful because it looks at people's reactions live on camera to particular situations deliberately set by the producers. One such moment was when they made their stuntman to fall as if sick on the pavement in the middle of the city. No one stopped to help him. One vagrant black woman stopped and asked 'man are you alright?' She started asking passers by, 'somebody help, call an ambulance.' No one paid attention. People passed by. She didn't leave. She continued, 'somebody help, call an ambulance.' Eventually one woman came, started to call for an ambulance and tried to help. The producers showed themselves up and gave interviews. The stunt man said something curious. He said while he laid there, the woman's voice kept calling. It was like an angel calling out. One psychologist interviewed on the programme said that the vagrant woman was indeed his angel. How true! After the producers revealed themselves, she kept asking the stuntman, 'are you alright man?' when he said yes. She went on her way.

The inflation rate in the country was running at double figures. In the 2000s, inflation in the country rose to plus 100 per cent. The economic deterioration was worsened by the total disregard to the peaceful laws that had always guided us in the country. My people are law abiding. The militants' takeover of white-owned commercial farms emboldened many petty thieves into full time intimidators. They totally disregarded the law of the land. The economic nose dive and subsequent crush later on in the years was man made. Four billion dollars unbudgeted was given to combatants of the seventies liberation war. My Grandma Chihwiza fought day and night, meditating and preparing cadres to go to the front. All she got was some dubious character taking over her fertile farm. The sudden DRC war contributed to the negative economy. The government sent troops to support the ailing government of Laurent Kabila in Congo. Soldiers prospered in those times. It was popular to hear 'he came back from DRC' being whispered and people would follow the guy around for free rounds of drinks. Corruption became the mainstay of the economy. Faiths sects sprouted all over the suburb. Every open space was being competed for by the faith sects, the urban farmers and the rogue bands of fake party youths. Hardship was everywhere. If it became too much to bear there was always a small faith sect at any one patch of ground you could go to and get solace.

My closest friend from school days joined the police force. He told me that when he went for traffic duty for the first time it was an eye opener. After the shift was over they went back to camp. They took showers and changed. All his friends were going to drink at the mess. He didn't have money. One of his colleagues asked him if he was going to join him. He replied he didn't have money. 'You are stupid George! How come you don't have money after the whole day in traffic duty?' From that day my friend became a suburban policeman eager to take bribes. Among his group he was known not to hesitate to receive money. He became efficient at collecting bribes. One day he followed up on one old man who was supposed to pay a bribe because his son had been let out of police custody. The man told his wife to tell George that he was not there. George sensed the lie and he said ok I will wait for him. He sat in the veranda until the old man came out. He apologised and paid up. He had adjusted to the realities of the times. He was a good cop. Environment turned him into a corrupt suburban policeman.

Suburban Police

I'm lean cut, I kick hard like a criminal cop,
My haircut fresh
Free of an ounce of donut fat,
Just brawn and blood steel rolled fresh
I got my clout and a roll of cash,
My badge, my Santana and an ounce on the dash
Crash the canon, bust Charlie, it's like a leash
I pocket tokens of profligacy in the flower park
Decretum sentinel, cavalier, crooked Dick
My word is behest, my boot to lick
I'm angular and I wallop multiple times
Careful, a clash may send you to the domicile of stiffs
Was straight and green yesterday, dry were my pockets
Beadledom ceded a solution, DIY, recalcitrant
Akin to a round cop in a square deal
I deal real
The finest, the ace cast cop that kick hard like a
    criminal cop

George used to enjoy teasing me so much. At times he suggested that we go and have a turn with the prostitutes who lined up near the Harare Kopje. He knew I wouldn't agree, so he first made a joke, 'Mbiramatako, do you know that people used to ask Jesus in amazement when he talked to prostitutes. They said you are divine do not touch them. Jesus would reply that he came exactly for those prostitutes!' Earlier, in school, we used to be very ambitious and especially me. I used to be strict in thinking that every man must make it in life. We finished school and I started work, George joined the police. We usually met for drinks. He always played the song by Gerry Rafferty, 'Baker's Street'. He looked at me with an eye that said 'used to think it was so easy, but is it?' and I just look at him, resignation written on my countenance.

The bleakness never stopped. I seemed to be getting deeper into the recesses of failure and confusion. I stopped work and asked for a package which was duly given. I was about to relocate to Europe with Godmother. She had an accident. Her company agreed to pay air ticket for me to go and see her. This was in pen and paper. I resigned took the package and built a house. In the meantime I processed my visa. It was straight forward. I was invited. Alas the Immigration rejected my visa. They considered my age as a flight risk and seek work illegally in the UK. I was stuck with no money and no job.

Things couldn't get any worse. My girlfriend gave birth to a beautiful baby girl. She was the only light in those bleak days. I did not intend it to happen like that. When God gives we say thank you. I was playing with our beautiful daughter in the lounge. Lord she looked beautiful. The skin smooth and healthy. She was smiling that innocent smile that knows no evil. Looking at her got me thinking about her future. I knew I was broke but I had to shelter my daughter and protect her. I decided to marry my girlfriend. Our daughter had a legitimate name and home.

We prepared for the wedding. We met a friendly magistrate. We ended up talking more. I told him that my visa application was denied. He offered that he could help with the visa application. All he needed was money. I went and borrowed from my friend who was running his own company. I added my own remaining cash and gave the old magistrate. He took our passports and told me to wait two weeks. Finally things seemed to be lighting up. At least he was a magistrate. I could trust him. We held the wedding. The vows at court went smoothly. The after party was great, with lots of liquor, beers and different meats and eats. It was awkward because my girlfriend's father never came to the event. Only my sister and mom graced the occasion. All my friends and a few neighbours attended. I didn't notice how strange it was.

I was in cloud nine, ready to jump on a journey. I started a fowl run at the back of the yard. It was primarily as a hobby. In the process I realised it was a good source of delicious organic chicken. Plus some cash on the side. It was the chickens' noise that woke me up as dawn broke. I rushed to take a bath. I went into town to meet the magistrate for our visas and passport. He came and told me that he could not process it. His link at the British embassy had been transferred. He told me to give him one more week while he sorted things out. One month turned to months until I reported to police. He denied everything. In the end it was my word against his word. He won. He was a magistrate! He punished me further by not returning our passports. When it rains it's always a downpour. Things never stopped getting worse.

The next turn of events stunned me. It all happened as if I was following a script. Our beautiful daughter got sick. We rushed her to emergency room. She became stable after a day admitted at the hospital. It happened twice again and the same physician attended to us. He advised me to check for HIV virus in our daughter. I was devastated. I was scared. At the same time I was reassured because we were checked when my girlfriend registered at the local maternity ward. Our daughter was tested and she was negative. That gave us hope.

One Saturday night I was at home drinking beer alone. My wife and kid had gone to sleep. I stayed very late drinking. I went out and topped up the beers. At 2 am, wife came running to the lounge. She told me our daughter had collapsed. I was intoxicated but I quickly sobered up. I went to my neighbour to ask for help with his car. We took our daughter to a faith healer at the suggestion of my wife. That was the morning I met her. The faith healer. She dressed in all white. She was light skinned with huge eyes. Her long black hair flowed perfectly down her shoulders. I felt intrigued to see her. She certainly had a different air about her. I didn't envisage our acquaintance to be a long one. She attended to our daughter. She looked at her for quite some time. The first words she uttered were, 'where is her grandmother?' She was referring to my mother. We told her that she was at her house. She did not say anything else. We stayed there for two days before going back to our own house. Our daughter was feeling better. Our daughter became sick again. We rushed her to hospital emergency department. They gave her emergency treatment and she was discharged. When she got the attack she would be unable to breath.

That same week the faith healer visited us. We told her what had happened the night before. She took our daughter into her arms and said, 'your daughter shall not go to hospital again.' Sure thing from that day we never took our beautiful daughter to hospital again. It became easy for us. Any cause of concern, we consulted the faith healer. We had backup. My wife suggested that we needed to visit another different faith healer in another part of town. My wife and my mother never saw face to face. They had similarities in their character. They were both deep believers in faith healers and witches. There was suspicion on the part of my wife since the faith healer had asked about my mother on our first visit. She took it to mean witchcraft and no one could convince her otherwise. Slowly we became incorporated into our faith healer's church. She was kind to us. She was a powerful woman. We became members of her church. She could see I was desperate to emigrate so she promised to help.

As the months passed we became senior members of the church. It was a young church. At one of the church sermon the faith healer announced that she had a dream. If we went overseas I would die. My dream died with her dream. The issue of emigrating was closed. I was stunned. My wife took it well. She settled into the church routine. I was an intelligent young man with work experience but loafing around. The faith healer gave me the role of secretary of the church. I was very reluctant. I didn't do much and she lightly chided me.

Eventually I worked for her. I started by organising her money to separate it from church and personal. I opened one account for church and one personal in her name. She used to get huge amounts of cash from happy people she helped. She was quite popular. I used to see popular sports writers and prominent football players visit her. African footballers are notorious for juju. I saw business executives and business men. I received the gifts and banked them in. During church sermons we collected the usual church offerings. I banked it in the church account. I went to lawyers and changed a dubious contract she had been made to sign. Where there is money crooks want to take advantage. Everything was now efficient, she was happy. I even organised a trip to our neighbouring country where they needed faith healing services. They were willing to pay.

I partially funded the trip. We arrived at our main client's house. He took us to the house he wanted cleansed of evil spirits. He was a businessman. We also cleansed his shop. He said we were to sleep at that house which needed cleansing. The homestead had two huts. It was in the rural area of that country. After cooking and eating we slept in separate huts. She slept in the hut with the red cloth which was believed to be the source of evil. I was tired from the long journey by bus and all day working. I immediately slept. I was awoken by the sound of the faith healer's voice, taunting. She seemed to be in argument and duel with something. I became numb with fear. I think some neighbours called police. A police patrol car came and flashed its lights. I rushed outside and full blast they put their lights in my face shouting for me to raise my hands. I did and they went inside my hut and looked around. They went to the faith healer's hut. She was sitting but looking very tired.

They asked her who was fighting. She said no one. They were intrigued. They thought they heard fighting. They searched around. Asked for our passports checked passes and they left. When they were gone she told me that the place was evil. Particularly the red cloth. The evil had attacked her. We didn't sleep again. We sat and talked till morning. The next day she had cold sores on her lips like she had suffered a severe headache. We went to stay in another village. We stayed at the same businessman's parents' house. We got a clean living house. We could cook our own food. It was much better. There was harmony. The faith healer taught me about life and how she thought things should be. The girls in that country are known for their beauty. At the house we were staying there was one young girl doing form three in school. She was very friendly. She grew a liking for my cooking. She came and three of us shared meals every night. It was good. People were coming for consultations. That meant money and gifts.

When we returned we became more involved in church. My mom became a member. I was happy that finally my wife and mom were unified in their faiths. My sisters thought it was a good thing. I was looking at it at the surface. What I didn't know was that the conflict would escalate. There were smiles on the surface only but deep resentment for each other. The faith healer was only human and took sides. A fire was smouldering. I was in strife. I was caught between the two most powerful and beloved women in my life. My mom and my wife. It was tension after tension. It was hard for me to pick sides. One night I had a dream where I was fighting my own mom. It was so vivid. The influence from the wife's side was really winning me over. I was about to turn against my mom. I became suspicious of her. I hinted to my sister who was staying with her that time. It was the darkest time of my life.

I was hopeless. The economic situation was not helping at all. It was a war zone within my family and in the country without a real war being fought. I was driven crazy by going from one faith sect to another. The crazy political decisions being made by the country's leaders were a pain in the neck. In the winter of May of that year the government surprised us by a hastily implemented 'operation cleanup.' They demolished all so called illegal structures. In truth they were the majority of people's homes. My back yard barbershop at my parents' house was demolished. My elder brother's son was making money from it. He became hopeless. The police patrolled the suburbs in armoured vehicles. They forced my brother's son to demolish the saloon. He sought help from friends. They used hammers to crush the barbershop. Dreams were crushed while police waited in armoured cars to enforce a painful law. My brother's son was the man at home. He looked after my mom. When his source of income was crushed he went to South Africa to look for work. My family was once again robbed of a son figure. The consequences of a people loving government.

Battle lines had been drawn. The opposition was calling for giving legal title to communal lands. To take back all land dubiously grabbed or given under resettlement scheme. They advocated for the utilization of all state land. The ruling party viewed land as people's resource. Land reform was its most important agenda. It noted that 6000 white farmers owned more than 70 per cent of the productive land in my country. The government wanted to solve unemployment by promoting local businesses. It aimed to encourage entrepreneurship in rural areas. In practice hordes of youth remained unemployed. It was routine for most young men to wake up and spend the whole day drinking at the local shopping centre. The number of bottle stores increased dramatically. I dreaded going to the local shop lot. Gangs of former school friends and boys who never worked since leaving high school pestered for money for alcohol. The government was deliberately keeping people drunk and useless.

Saturday morning, I had a hung over. Nothing new but this one was heavy. I had slept at 3 am, now 6 am, my wife was calling already for me to get up and get going. Prepare for church 150 km away by bus. I wasn't up to it. She became very cross. She proceeded to prepare and went to church. I slept on for another hour before waking up. I took a shower. I remembered my mom said she wanted to see me after church. I had been baptised at the Great River that roars and rumbles through the Eastern part of my country. The bridge in the main highway crossing that great river was the spot of many accident disasters. Mom also got baptised in the same river but on a different day when I was not in attendance. I remember my wife describing mom's baptism to me. She laughed and mimicked how my mom had gone into a trance. She delighted in how the faith healer kept whipping mom with generous amounts of the great river water. I didn't know how to react. I curiously thought, 'does she know that's my mother she is talking about?' she had become complacent.

I had become complacent with God. On this particular Saturday instead of going to worship I proceeded to get plastered. I found my way to my mom's place. It was 8 pm, she was back from church. She asked me why I had not gone to church. I told her I wasn't feeling well. 'But you are drunk?' she asked again. I told her that my illness needed some beer to cure. She gave me dinner. She told me she wanted to go to another faith healing sect in a remote area of the country. I was stunned. I thought she had converted to our church. I was intoxicated. I felt not in the mood to argue. I also felt for her. I could see the insecurity deep down.

I guess every mother knows the pain of losing an only son to the influence of the wife. Coupled with maternal love will be a deep belief that someone was out there to harm us spiritually. So I agreed. We fixed the date for the next weekend. The next weekend I prepared and collected mom. We used the bus. We went as a group with other faith believers of that sect. We had all contributed and hired one bus. We reached the village by sunset. We camped alongside others who were already there. The rule at the sect was that men and women should always be separated. Men slept on the other side and women on the other. The only person I knew in that sect was my mom. We separated as required. I asked around to find where men from my town were. I was shown. I unpacked, put out my blanket and lay down on the grass. The men around looked at me. I looked different. I was dressed in Lee jeans and t shirt. I went to the bush nearby to pass urine. I came back and I saw one of the men with a stick throwing away my blanket and bag. I confronted him. They all grouped around me. I thought about my mom. I picked up my staff and went to another place near the women. I observing the allowed distance and slept there.

What struck me was the location. It was set at a rough patch of land with hard shrubs and trees that looked lifeless. Donkeys were the only animals I saw. That part of the country was dry. Despite the rough conditions I didn't feel discomfort. I was floating in a gentle haze. At night my dreams were very peaceful. I didn't remember them in the morning. I felt the peace linger. Whilst I was there I never felt craving for smoking.

Township life is amazing. Every town has a witch doctor practising. I encountered one. At times I think that the witch doctors could be incorporated into main stream science or social sciences programmes. One day burglars stole my VCR recorder and new cell phone from my house. My neighbours suggested that I go and see a certain witch doctor. They gave me directions. I went and I encountered her sitting under a mango tree outside the house. She was prospering. I saw trucks of sand off loading. She was building. I told her my problem. She replied me, 'I can help you to see the thief. You drink my concoction and go inside that room and look at the white paper. You will see your thief.' I was incredulous. She continued, 'my medicine is very powerful. It can show you anything you want. It can show you your dead relatives or Jesus Christ.' I pondered awhile. 'The problem is you don't believe yet thieves come here to get medicine to steal successfully' I said let me try. I paid five dollars local currency. She gave me half a cup of the liquid, brownish in colour. I took the entire amount in one go. She told me to wait five minutes.

In about three minutes I felt like I was drunk. I told her and she said go to the room. I went inside the dark room. I looked at the white paper. Images started to appear, at first disjointed. Unstable moving about. At one time I saw only the eye. It was like the image was elusive. At last it clicked and stabilised. I felt like I was walking outside. I saw the tall friend from my next door. It was like I was walking beside him. We were entering the suburb together. The clear outline of the suburb was real. The friend was bald. Before I left him with hair. I came out stunned. It was so real. She gave me roots and said as soon as I reach home I burnt the roots. The thief would come to me. I didn't like the lingering effect of the medicine. I kept hearing faint voices of people speaking as if from far, as if in conference. I went home and burnt the roots. Before they were burnt out the tall friend visited. I was shocked. He asked me what I was doing. I asked him what he had done.

I didn't see the emergency that needed so many churches. Our daughter was completely healed. She never fell sick again. I felt it was time to break ties with the faith healer's church. My wife was deeply devoted. She did not favour the idea of quitting. There was always a flurry of activity around me. I preferred to be alone. I was trying to think straight. I didn't have a job. I drifted apart from everyone. My mom, my wife and other close family members. The harder the situation became the more my wife went deeper into faith and faith healers. I couldn't think straight. I was surrounded by people who didn't understand me. My neighbours saw me but they never knew the shattered dreams, the pain I was bearing.

I never meant my life to be that low. Surrounded by people who were satisfied by small every day things. I wanted more. I needed wide open spaces. I wished for a change in my life. I hated small thinking. My wife was prone to small thinking. It is often believed that a charm can be effective to make the husband loyal and loving. Faith healers also claim to be able to make the husband loyal and loving. I'm not sure what drove my wife to try these methods to spice up our marriage. She consulted a faith healer. He told her to

bring my favourite shirt for charming. The aim was that when I wore
the shirt, instant love for my wife will ensue. I thought I already loved
my wife! She quietly took my Van Huesen shirt to the healer brought
it back and put it in the wardrobe. I continued to wear it without
inkling. Women in the neighbourhood share intimate details. My wife
forgot to take a charm to keep her friends quiet. Soon all the women
knew. They told my family. My family informed me. It didn't matter
much to me. Later on reflection I saw how I was involved in real
low society if there is one. Romance was believed to be enhanced
through charms and faith healing. I understood attraction in terms
of beauty and appeal. What I needed was to escape the ignorant web
that was being spun around me by the society I was living in.

At this moment in my life I reached one of the most painful
decisions. I decided to divorce my wife or at least separate, anything to
give me a break and reorient my self. I informed all my close relatives.
I went to my in laws and informed them of my decision. They
accepted and told me that should I change my mind I was welcome
back. I thanked them. I was free! Though I was very sad. Especially
when I thought of my daughter, I never missed the mother. I used to
go and see her. I put money in her account whenever I had it.

The moment I was alone I thought on my feet. There was no
pressure to go to church from my wife. The pressure from my mom
eased. She left me alone. She reprimanded me when the drinking
got heavy. I was drinking quite heavily, but I was clear minded. I
started looking around for a new fresh start. I went into town daily.
Nothing came. I thought of going back to college. Enrol in a skills
based course, nursing. In my country there are only government
hospital nursing schools offering nursing course. Godmother has a
very special friend. One who is always there for her. I am grateful
to Godmother's friend. She's my own sister. I never forget where
we've come from. Her husband was very knowledgeable. He stayed
in Europe most of his working life. He has since passed on. May
God bless his soul. I told him I wanted to go back to college but no
place. He said to me, 'Go East young man.' He suggested that I try

China. He gave me the agency dealing with that. I went there and my qualifications were accepted by one University in China. The agency facilitated everything including my first semester fees. My other sister agreed to have them deduct the amount over one year plus their service charges. They agreed to this because of the trust in our family friend. Suddenly I was ready to fly to China. It happened so fast. The application to University, acceptance and we were invited to the Chinese embassy to be given orientation. Some came with their parents. I was alone. I met one girl there, a teacher and we became friends. R. Kelly song, 'The Storm is Over Now' comes to mind. The storm was finally over. At least there was a new beginning right there!

In every young man's life there comes a time when you have to sacrifice it all. Go for the war of your life. I flew on my country flight which passed through Malawi Singapore and finally China, Beijing. At the airport everyone formed a queue and they went through. My turn came. The officer went through all my papers. He put them all together took my passport and was about to stamp. He rummaged my papers again and said, 'where return ticket?' I was stuck. I had skipped buying return ticket because my money was not enough. I thought it was not a big deal because I had proof that I was going to study. Immigration law did not work like that. I was pulled from the queue and taken to an office. The supervisor asked if I had money to buy a return ticket right there at the airport. I told him to try. He came back and told me it cost a lot of US dollars. No way. I was lost. They made the decision that I could try to find money from friends or relatives and buy a ticket. Or they were putting me back on the next plane home. I went out of the office and wandered around in front of the immigration counter. My mind was in turmoil. New arrivals came and formed a new queue. The officers had switched. It was a young beautiful girl there. I decided to join the queue and try. She took my papers and passport. She asked me how much money I had for upkeep. I told her. She stamped my passport and let me through. I had made it, thank you Lord.

I reached my college hostel and slept. The next morning I went to the Medical University, Dept of Nursing studies. I enrolled and while I was enrolling the principal looked at my qualifications and age. He suggested I do degree straight. I didn't have enough finance. I settled for Diploma in nursing studies. The next day I went for orientation. I met my classmates. Monday classes started. After ten years since I left high school, I was a student again! It was hard. I was a mature face among fresh young girls 18 to 23 years. I was 30, God! God is wonderful, I did my best to assimilate. I smoked less, went for gym and studied hard. I participated in class. I was grateful. The class accepted me without much drama. The Indian workers at the food court gave me a hard time. They mocked me and asked if I was student or lecturer. I stood out. My built which is big, my skin colour and age. I was a thorn among roses. Lecturers were professional. They didn't give much notice to my age in class. In private I am sure they talked about me. I was different. One Chinese lecturer who was very bright and eccentric asked 'Do we have any middle aged student here?' All 89 pairs of eyes in the lecture theatre automatically shifted to me. I have a peculiar habit. When I am stressed up I softly scratch my forehead. Stress being my constant companion the damage to the skin on my forehead was immense. On top of that I used to suffer heat rush. The forehead was itchy and I scratched. My forehead showed a badge that reflected time, hard time. The spots on the forehead increased my age by ten years! I looked old in that class of fresh faced pale young girls. I noticed that society here was very polite. Some were grumpy and showed sour faces. Those who were friendly invited me for a cup of tea or coffee at the local coffee shop. They eat for fun. My guiding principle in dealing with local people was very simple. I got that advice from Godmother's closest friend. She told me, 'Mbiramatako don't try to lead people in their own country. Know always why you travelled there. Respect differences.' What wise counsel. Until today it works for me. I never try to lead people in their turf. They have their own pride and customs.

My primary class consisted of 82 girls and 7 boys. In practical sessions we divided into smaller teams of ten students each group. My world was full of women.

Classes were held at the university. Practical simulations were done in the laboratory at the university. Practical sessions were done at the general hospital. Practical was interesting. I got to meet and interact with different individuals from different walks of life. There was one patient who lay in bed. He was surrounded by wide eyed students. He said 'my system reversed on me. Instead of passing shit the normal way I vomited my shit through my mouth for one month.' Another patient told us that he hadn't slept for eight years. 'So what do you do at night? And how do you feel generally?' Vlarena was keen to know. The patient replied that at night he just lay down. He said generally he felt lousy. During my first semester practical. It was very hard for me to ask the patients if they had opened bowels and urine. I observed experienced nurses briskly ask more intimate questions without blinking. I learnt the personal nature of my chosen profession. I experienced my first sight of a huge bedsore that covered the entire buttocks of a patient. I wondered where to start doing the dressing from. It was huge.

In my fifth semester I did community nursing. I assisted in child birth. I assisted a young woman. She had trouble pushing out. The husband arrived, held her hand. He cried in agony with her. She pushed and the baby was out. It was an intense moment for me. I'm not sure how to describe the feeling. I felt a profound emotion watching a new life come out. In my procedure requirements I was mandated to do vaginal swabbing. Most females were reluctant to have males perform on them. I was lucky to have a vibrant clinical instructor. She picked out a lady teacher. She explained my need to perform the procedure. The lady was very intelligent. She allowed me to perform the procedure. I was the only male in my group. All my colleagues were smiling at me as I prepared my trolley. I performed without incident. I thanked the lady. When I performed the procedure I understood the word anatomy. It was an anatomy playing an important function in creation.

I was surprised to meet quite a number of prominent people's children in China. I am naïve. I still find it astonishing that leaders including my President send their children outside for education. At home politicians told us that ours was the best education system. I'm not against their children learning overseas. They could build excellent schools for those at home. The excellent schools can attract other foreign students. Enabling exposure to international trends and foreign currency earnings.

I flew to China to study nursing. The government can provide more nursing schools at home. I flew to China in desperation for education. Their kids flew to China out for variety. The best money can offer. Politicians in my country tend to exist in perpetual power duels that ignore the people. They're good at spending money among connected elites. A wise man who finds power must use the power to give people a decent existence. He provides people clean water, electricity, education, jobs, access to technology etc plus sovereignty. The present crop of politicians in my country is good at preaching sovereignty to starving people. Before people taste and savour that sovereignty, they will be dead from hunger, disease and political violence. No need to try to hoodwink people about sovereignty. While behind stealing everything. Go ahead steal. Do not starve the people. You can't have it all! The art of balancing between stealing and giving some to the people is largely lacking among leaders in my country.

Africans are the least respected on the international scene. My friend was jailed in a foreign country. He was shocked to find people from other nations having representatives from their countries assisting them to get out. From Africa no officials were helping. I read in local dailies about Africans getting killed in street violence with locals. And having illegal post mortems done. Why is this done to Africans? Our base is weak. When I have conversations with fellow Africans, the tune is the same, 'they don't like us, these people!' 'They exploited us and they put up laws to keep us down!' I always say that its time for every disadvantaged African to stop blaming anyone. Stop looking for anything from anyone and focus on the foundations. Accept our weakness that the other man somehow managed to buy and sell our ancestors. That was in the past. Somehow we happen to constitute among the most poor, that also is not important because we have smart brains. What we lack is the formula and initiative to be original in the use of that brain. We spend our time and effort trying to compete against established domains. Stop the rat race. Let's get rid of futile mode. Let's be reborn within our individual selves. Grandma Chihwiza was correct when she said that the imperialist trapped people by material things. Long ago we survived in harmony and sweet bliss without sugar. Presently we tasted the material world. We have become enslaved. The old song that Africa must unite is not functional. The tune to dance to is Africa Innovate! In innovation lies development.

At times the African man is too loud for comfort. Many a time the taxi drivers complain. Two friends he picked up sat right next to each other and shouted at each other all the way. We like drink and loud music. We board the plane from very far away to disturb people with loud rhumba music. Very often we fight and shout over women. We are prone to behave exactly the same way we behave at home. When Africans became rich through internet scams it blew. Every wannabe journalist wanted to cover that. Some made trips to Africa to catch offenders red handed. That's the result of African swagger. Russians have been dealing billions in illicit gains for decades but no one talks about it. They are quiet. I have seen fellow Africans invite a huge team of friends for a drink at the club. One man buying for the whole mob, incredible. Or just hold an impromptu party where champagne is used to wash hands. The loud boasting is amped up. All that nonsense gives the game away. A locale hath got eyes and ears! Next time they see me with my girlfriend having a drink, 'crook' goes in their mind but I am no crook. Africans, we are good. We are set for great things ahead. Attitude is the hardest to change. Let's have less lyrics and more depth. Still waters run deep.

When I got exposed to the international arena, where I met different nationalities, one pattern came out. Every one is excellent at detecting the speck in another's eye. They never see the log in their own eyes. One day I sat with my friend from Saudi Arabia. We watched 50 cent music video. He commented on 50 cent's jewellery saying it's so expensive. He said 'Why doesn't he help other blacks instead of wearing expensive jewellery?' I replied him, 'do you know how many brown people are living in abject poverty, yet one crown prince is building islands in the sea from scratch!'

There is something sinister and deliberate about labelling people according to colour. This colour reins supreme, that one, ok because it's near the supreme one and this one is a no no, too much melanin! As this colour as sin, as this colour as death. On the wings of a supreme coloured dove. I observed something peculiar, local women here, whom I perceived as perfectly pretty thought that they needed to be whiter. They use whitening creams. I found out that even the mental patients at the hospital, the uneducated labourers in restaurants, in the malls and the toilet cleaners will belittle anyone who looks darker than them. Labelling humans according to colour is a very powerful tool. Incompetent individuals hope to get power and leverage from it.

I met characters who thought they were the elite, they just felt that way. They started to believe it. There was one man I met and apparently he gave himself the name Droc because of his academic brilliance. He was doing masters in psychology. He was ever ready to go into details about it. How important his decisions would be if he was employed in a company. One day I met him in the morning. He asked where I was going. I told him to college. 'College, for what?' he asked 'What is done in college?' I asked back, 'I am doing my degree there'. I told him. 'Degree, you?' he asked and really looked perplexed as if only certain people can do it. Oh, stop being so full of it.

I noticed something about one guy who came to stay with me as my housemate. He was a nice intelligent guy. I didn't see any problem with him until I noticed his keenness to talk to my girlfriend. My girlfriend was Mor. I am not sure what sort of attraction forces was happening. Maybe my girlfriend was flirty. The guy took every opportunity to talk to her. If he needed to give me something he gave through her. When he went to his country and was about to return he sent a message direct to Mor instructing her to keep his keys for him. One day I was back from work. My girl was at work. He would usually be in his room all day with the light off; because of the position of his room it was always dark. I was wearing my girlfriend's slippers. I moved about the house. Probably he could hear the squishing sound the slippers. He opened right on time when I was at his door. He was in his underwear. He looked stunned. He could not utter a word. He closed the door. 'Hey bro, what's up?' I shouted to him. He had bolted the door. Reminded me of South African singer Lucky Dube's song, 'My brother, my enemy.'

I met people who tried to convince me to repent. Reorient and be born again but not as persistent as this sister. We stayed in the same area. She had a car. She gave me a lift daily. This gave her ample opportunity to persist. After classes at college she told me and my girlfriend to go to her house. She said there was a function there. I never suspected that it was a prayer meeting. We reached her unit. I was confused. There was a lot of nice food. The sister was dressed in a tank top that left the navel out and a pair of jeans. Not only that pair of jeans had we seen that night, as we waited for others to come, she changed clothes twice more. Each time she was really nicely dressed.

Finally she came with a bible. It dawned on me that this was actually a church service! All went well. The Pastor who was male had a disturbing knack of talking and laughing loudly. He opened up the sermon by saying we were all kings. I wondered, 'are we really kings?' Everyone was laughing! Oh oops. I'd thought aloud. The pastor was annoyed slightly. He explained where he was coming from. He ended by saying that he was better than any king. He could heal whereas kings could only rule. Oh . . .

CHAPTER 5

Amazing how time flies. Before I knew it I was doing my last practical at the general hospital in Beijing. We followed the staff shift from 7 am to 2pm. After 2 pm I went home to the Condo and slept. I woke up at 5 pm and went for gym. Gym helped me a lot to cope physically. I made sure I partake every free time. I attended University and did part time shift. I made sandwiches in front of customers at the mall. In healthcare there are life and death situations that bind work colleagues closer together. You develop a natural trust for each other. This is true of me and Vlarena. I and Vlarena were paired to look after an elderly patient with Parkinson disease. He was on tube feeding before. He could eat and swallow soft food. The old man was very restless. He craved to eat bread his family had brought earlier. 'Can I give him?' Vlarena asked me. I'd seen the man eat bread tossed in milk. I suggested doing the same. Vlarena proceeded to give the wetted bread. The old man ate the first morsel of bread. The second got stuck. He coughed and immediately his face turned blue! We learnt in college blue meant no oxygen. We could lose the old guy. We panicked. I wasn't thinking anymore. I went behind him and wrapped my arms around him. I thrust inwards with all my power. Instantly a lump of bread popped out of the patient's mouth. He stopped struggling. He was relieved. I was sweating. Vlarena had tears in her eyes.

We stayed at the same Condominium. A block away from each other. It was easy for her and her boyfriend Leong to visit me. We did most of our home work together. I struck up conversation with Vlarena during tea break. 'You know I went to your country when I was five years old. Our parents were tobacco merchants. They did business in your country. We went together with my sister.' Vlarena informed me. 'Are you serous? Do you remember how it was like?' I asked as I sipped my coffee. 'Now it's all a blur, but my parents were always there before they retired to Hong Kong.' Vlarena said and looked at me with her huge soft eyes. I was intrigued. Why Hong Kong, I was surprised. 'Well mainly because all our roots are there, so my parents felt more comfortable there. And you know my father told me he made very good friends with your President. He said your president was a great man who gave his people land. He also said your country's government like my father because my father and other merchants broke the tradition of a cartel fixing the tobacco prices.' Vlarena flicked a lock of hair into place and said 'its time up lets go back to work.'

Friday afternoon, we were just about to finish at the psychiatry ward. We sat at the long bench awaiting our clinical instructor to dismiss us. This was the last day of practical. We were given one week holiday before we began final preparations for the university exams and the nursing board exams. Vlarena turned to me. She said 'today is Friday Mbiramatako, let's go out and drink.' I asked about money. I was broke. In the end none of us had money to go out. We went home and separated at the condo. I reached took a shower and did my homework. I didn't have enough money to go out. I had for one bottle of Chivas at the liquor store. It was cheaper going to the club. I called Vlarena. I suggested that we buy one bottle and hang out in my apartment. She agreed and came with Leong. We opened the bottle. We drank and watched TV. A 100-year-old runner became the oldest person to complete a full-distance marathon when he finished the race in Toronto on the previous Sunday. 'If the mind is set nothing can stop an individual', I commented. 'Yap the mind is powerful. You should see my sister. She is brilliant and strong willed. She can do anything' agreed Vlarena. I chuckled, 'come on, no one can do anything they want, there are limits!' 'You will meet her' said Vlarena seriously. It sounded like a warning to me. Soon we forgot about the conversation. We partook and broke off when all the liquor was finished. They said bye. I slept.

At the university a rumour went that the two sisters were lesbian. A lot of rumours flew around about Vlarena and Mei. I didn't follow them. The next night I was practicing rhyme inside my room. I had Bernard Shaw with me to inspire. Ding dong went the bell. I strode to the door and opened, Leong and Vlarena were at the door waiting expectantly. They burst into the room leaving me to slam the door shut and follow them. They led straight to my room. I shouted, 'hey, hey who is the owner of the house here?' we all laughed and went inside. They both dived onto the bed. 'I am so tired, work' yawned Vlarena. They relaxed Leong was tall and thin. He was handsome with a stub of a beard on his chin. He wore spectacles. He looked like a geek. Vlarena told me to open the brown package they had brought. Inside there was one bottle of Chivas, they knew it was my favourite. There was one roasted duck and sauce. 'Lovely' I said as I went out. I brought glasses knife and plate. We all sat down on the carpet. We sipped and feasted.

The mbira is a traditional music instrument in my country. I knew its power when I stayed at Chihwiza farm. The melody evokes trance states in spirit mediums. Grandma Chihwiza gave me my own mbira instrument when I was five years old. I looked after it as my talisman. She also gave me the zebra mask. Whenever Leong and Vlarena came to my house I played the mbira. They enjoyed its harmony but not as much as Mei did when she joined us later on. I went and brought out my African mask and donned it. I played the mbira. I loved my zebra mask. My grandma Chihwiza had given it to me. I shook my head from side to side as I played sweet spiritual music from the mbira. Leong and Vlarena laughed until their eyes watered. They also tried it on. Later we were taken by the merry waters and tired so we broke off the party. I yawned and went on to finish the remaining liquor before going to sleep.

We turned our attention to study. We worked hard. Vlarena came to my apartment every night. We practiced using past exam questions. We exchanged the work and marked for each other. At times we studied until after midnight. We were faced with university exams plus Nursing board exams. We both passed both exams. Quite a number of our colleagues failed. They had to repeat. Vlarena and I were already looking forward to convocation. 'I wish my sister was coming to my graduation' Vlarena was sad. 'Where is she?' I asked her. 'She's in Chiang Mai. She's doing her art tutorship.' 'I thought you said she's a doctor?' 'Yes she did her MBBS in Hong Kong. She practiced there for two years before moving to China. She stopped two years ago. She went to Chiang Mai to study art under the tutorship of an old family friend. She's nearly through with her tutorship.' We booked gowns and caps at the University. We attended rehearsals for the event. On the big day, I hired a car. We took Leong along. The venue was full of proud parents and relatives. We received our diplomas in nursing. I took a photo with Vlarena. The whole batch took a group photo. After convocation Vlarena got a job with the government general hospital. I was facing the daunting task of looking for a job.

The next morning I woke up with a headache and heartache. My spirit was restless. I was back at square one. The memories of unemployment came back. I had tried all I could. I couldn't get a job. I attended interviews with Singapore hospitals. It was in vain. Two main reasons were given, experience and foreign visa requirement. Eventually I headed backwards. When you hit a wall don't despair. Sometimes it helps to retrace and look for solutions in the past. I thought of one doctor whom I had trained under during my practical in the capital. I went to his ward and was received by the sister in charge and the general manager.

They were not sure how to treat me. They were kind enough to give me forms of employment to fill in. The doctor came. I told him the purpose of my visit. He was reluctant. He told me to try my embassy for help with work visa. I knew my embassy wouldn't help me to secure a job. It was not part of their obligation to me. I managed to convince him to try me for three months then I move on. The three months would be post basic training. He agreed to that as long I had a support letter from my university. The director of nursing at the University was a very professional lady. She agreed to give me a letter.

I started work with the general hospital. It was boot camp where everyone shouted and no one listened. If I managed to talk. It was horrible. The supervising nurse was very hostile. Whenever I stumbled, which was a lot of times, she would be right there inches from my neck. Observing, she was the inspector. Sometimes she was outright abusive in the local dialect. I didn't understand but instinctively I could tell she was scolding me. Bad words sound bad in every language. The doctor was a wise man. Honed and matured in knowledge of medicine. He was strict in maintaining standards. He was humane in dealing with life situation problems. He allowed possibilities. The rest was left to the individual to fulfil and achieve whatever they aspired for. I was lucky to meet that man. After the three months were over I asked to extend. He agreed but said I should renew my letter with the university. The University agreed again. I was on my way to a journey of nearly three years working at that hospital. I became eligible to enrol in degree programme.

Meanwhile me, Leong and Vlarena spent most of our free time together. They were either at work, or with me. I knocked off from the hospital. I was going home. My phone rang. Vlarena wanted to know about the two rooms in my apartment. My housemates had finished their work contract. They were shifting out. I offered Leong and Mei to take the rooms. She confirmed that she was taking one for herself and one for Mei. 'Oh your sister will be coming?' I asked. 'Yes she confirmed. She'll be coming back next month.' Vlarena replied. We hung up. By the beginning of the next month Vlarena shifted into the apartment. The other room was furnished and reserved for Mei. I found out that Mei and Vlarena were close. Vlarena never tired of talking about Mei. I asked her, 'You and Leong seem to be really serious. Are you going to get married?' 'Yes Mei said we have to get married because she knows how much I love him. He's the one who took away my virginity. My sister is very strict, she has never had sex with a man' Vlarena told me. 'We sometimes touch each other just for fun when we are lonely but I have Leong, we cannot do that. We grew up very close with my sister. My sister is a fierce liberal but very conservative also in a way. She is a puzzle to me. I don't know what she wants in life. When she comes back she plans to stay in the house and paint only. She plays the flute very well.'

Life was flowing in what I considered a normal way. I was working at the hospital. I stayed there and went back to the condo when I was off. My life was very regular. It revolved around work and my two friends, Leong and Vlarena. Sometimes we went out or just chilled at home. Sometimes I spent time with my girlfriend Mor. A month passed like this. It was lunch time. I was having my lunch break at the staff kitchen. My phone rang. Vlarena was on the line to tell me her sister had arrived. She was at the house already. 'Ok I look forward to meet her. I will be coming this Friday.'

That Friday I knocked off at two pm. I was off the whole weekend. I went to the apartment. I was a little nervous. I was more curious about Mei. I reached took out my key to open the door. The door was swung open. There stood Leong smiling sheepishly looking at my face which showed horrible disbelief. I heard a very sweet melody from a flute. I stepped inside. I turned to Leong as he closed the door. 'What the f word is this man? Who painted the lounge purple? And the bells? The alluring flute music? Are we having a wedding?' Leong did not answer me. He indicated. I looked in that direction. I saw her immediately. It was like a soft fire enveloped her. Probably I was having optical illusions. What with the purple walls and ceiling that imitated ring like pond water. I was a bit unsteady on my feet. I managed a good stride. I offered my hand.

She gave me a soft pale thin fingered hand. The grip was surprising firm. I looked directly in her eyes. Her eyes were beautiful big and ordinary. The gaze was not. She held me in that gaze. I felt hot. 'I'm Mbiramatako, how do you do?' I greeted her. I'm fantastic, my name is Mei, Vlarena's sister. I was named Mei coz I was born in the month of May.' she replied with such clarity of voice it was like the first time to hear someone talk to me. 'Oh I was also born in May! What a coincidence. You play the flute?' I asked. 'Yes for as long as I can remember I have played the flute' 'I'm going to take a shower, please excuse me.' I said as I exited. 'My pleasure' she replied.

Inside my room I closed the door and dove into my bed. 'God she is exquisite!' I stood up took my mask and put it on. I gyrated, whispering, 'good times are here again! Yes sometimes they come back!' I wasn't making sense. I was ecstatic. The door flew open. Mei stood there with my bag. 'You forgot your bag in the lounge. You're coming from work right, hope your bag is clean. What are you wearing?' she asked indicating the mask. I took off my zebra mask. I took my bag from her. Mei showed interest in my mask. She held it as she stepped into my room. She looked at me. I stared back. I was looking at her in the decent light of my room. She was an enigmatic beautiful young lady. She wore a night dress, very sheer it left everything outlined. I could trace my eyes to her pink small panties. 'The she goat goes to give birth near people so that the dogs can be set upon it.' She sensed my eyes on her. She shivered. She wrapped her small hands around herself. She continued to stare at me. As a diversion I asked, 'you don't knock?' I took back my mask. She backed away with the mask. She shouted softly, 'yin yang!' I didn't understand her. She gave me back my mask. She quickly walked out. I was left thinking 'oh God, this is weird.'

I came out of my room. I was confronted by the change in the apartment. The walls were painted in pale purple that became a deeper purple upwards. The ceiling was not spared, same purple colour. The lace curtains and new pink coloured curtains. There was a faint fresh smell of flowers. Two new chandeliers donned each end of the lounge. The bells were quite spectacular. Small bells that hummed sweetly according to the blow of wind in the house. Later Mei told me the bells were called Feng-ling in Chinese. I felt goose bumps on the flesh of my biceps. God it was weird alright. It was intensely harmonizing and sexy. I admitted to myself the house felt good to be in. Vlarena came out and explained to me that her sister arrived three days ago. She immediately requested to change the lounge. 'I couldn't stop her, she's very stubborn, besides she's an artist' Vlarena tried to explain. 'So how about the bills for the artistic impression, who will pay? I'm sure this all cost' I asked Vlarena. 'Don't worry about that, Mei has settled everything already. She can afford it. Remember she is an artist.' 'Artist again, it seems you let her get away with everything because she is an artist. Is she a celebrated artist or rich artist?' I wanted to know. 'She's neither rich according to what you think nor is she famous. She's a respected artist.' That night dinner was wonderful. We all helped to prepare dinner of rice, chicken and veggie. We put on music and opened the bottle. Soon we were all tipsy and hugely hungry. We tucked into the chicken. I called the supermarket downstairs to bring extra beers. We were on our way. The two girls were real guzzlers. They never sat still. 'I thought that Africans were dangerous!' rang out loud and clear. We froze. All everyone looked at me. I quickly said 'so what do you think now?' I know that people are individuals. Not race.' Leong said. The tension was broke. Mei shouted, 'bring out the mask!' 'And the mbira!' Vlarena suggested

I brought my talisman and mask out. We took turns to dance wearing it. Mei had never seen the mbira before. I strummed it in low vibes increasing the tempo as everyone got absorbed. She was intrigued. The mask and the melody of the mbira brought out something in me. I wanted to smoke weed. My friends did not know that I smoked. I kept it that way. I was faced with a very awkward situation, I needed my joint. I took advantage of the recently acquired camaraderie between me and Leong. I asked him to come aside with me. I proceeded to roll my joint while I pretended to be interested in his IT degree that he had just finished. I lighted it dragged and offered it to him. I expected him to refuse. He took it and smoked it. We exchanged it and before we were halfway, the girls screamed in concern, 'don't smoke weed in here!' Leong just stared at them. I think it had hit him already. He giggled continuously. I quickly went to the bathroom. I finished it washed my hands rinsed my mouth and went back. No one mentioned it again. We continued to drink. Before 4 am we were all joyfully numb from the liquor. The next day we laughed as we viewed the video we had taken.

Monday morning I was back at work. The week flew. I tried to put Mei out of my mind. Every time I relaxed my thoughts wandered to her. 'Exquisite' my brain kept repeating that word. She was beautiful and cool. The whole weekend she had behaved normally to me. I felt she was showing me that she took me like her brother? My thoughts were in turmoil. I had to take a break from my work to attend my fourth semester class. I went to the apartment. There was no one. I went in and settled. I was trying to be like everyone else around. My friends had girlfriends went out and got plastered. If there was a new chick in town they pursued. When Mei came I wanted to ask her out but I had my girlfriend Mor. I respected Mor. I didn't want to involve her in any conflict of interest. I kept a low profile. Mor was my workmate at the restaurant where I worked part time. Our relationship had started over half a year already. One day she asked me if I had a girlfriend. I told her no. She kept quiet. It took me one whole month before it dawned on me that she might be interested to go out with me. I asked her out and she agreed. It was a very special time for me to take out this gorgeous lady. She looked serious most of the time. She appreciated my character and opened up to me. Eventually she gave me her number. She didn't trust easily.

This day I finished my shift at 1 pm at the restaurant. It was a slow weekend. Mor was coming but much later. I went up to my unit and took a shower I lighted my laptop scrolled to YouTube. I put Bob Marley song 'Stir it up' I was thinking, 'oh man life is tough and all that, but with Bob on the turntable, it was gonna be alright.' My pleasure stick became very rock hard. I stood up and yawned. I could see my mister straining against my boxers. It really made me look and feel very potent. What with my lean body and abs, not exactly six packs but I was nearly there.

I had a new tattoo. I was sexy and I knew it! I went to the bathroom, took a piss and dived into bed, my usual style of getting into bed. I was sure I did damage to the bed. I was not a small man. I needed to rest for a while. I heard the door bell ring. Vlarena opened and let Mor in. she knocked and entered. She wore one of her normal dress. Her full mane of lustrous black hair was simply let down into a black flame on her shoulders. She looked intensely erotic. She wore no makeup. The lips cherry red alluring for a deep kiss. She looked most beautiful! I had seen her wearing this dress before. I'd not noticed how it discreetly clung to her shapely figure. It brought out the outline of her sheer tongs inside, it was innocently sexy, I needed to quench a fire in both of us. I saw something in her eyes before I realised I was in my boxers only. My member had solidified. It was knobby and heavy as if made from clay. It snuggled heavily within my boxers. I fumbled for my shorts. I had carelessly tossed them earlier. I couldn't find my shorts. She said never mind. In her move to reassure me she gestured with her hands. She mistakenly hit my clay oblong with a satisfying thud. I doubled up in mock pain. She came and wrapped her delicate small arms around me. She tried to make me stand. As I stood her dress gathered around her and became tight against her butt. I saw a clear outline of her very brief panties black in colour. I couldn't help it. I sighed sharply. She looked up at me. Her eyelids were heavy covering huge soft eyes. She did not move one inch. She looked in my eyes. I moved closer into her open arms.

A man got to do what a man got to do. I took off her dress. I looked at her crotch and the small black thing of panties. God black is potent. The panties' black colour made a daring beautiful contrast against her smooth skin. I took it off. She was in her most natural glory. I traced the outline of her body with my hot palms. She moaned softly opening her lips slightly. I immediately kissed her. I proceeded to take out my boner right on the spot. Still standing. Rearwards I gently eased my massive oblong into her hot broil. I started stirring upwards. No foreplay. She was quite wet. I stirred, thrust, cork screwed and hilted against her generous rump. I waited like that savouring the quick series of small contractions from her core. She was breathing fast. Her stomach fluttered continuously. I crooned to her in small sweet tones. I gently probed her to answer. When she tried she just gasped. The more she tried to control the spasms, the more her stomach fluttered. I felt juice well down my eager tool. I gently withdrew and laid her on the bed. I sucked her nipples going down. I reached her fire. I nibbled at it concentrating on the bean that eagerly sprung out of its soft folds. I rose and faced her. My heavy dong in my hand. She lay on the bed her eyes closed. Her legs wide open. With my hand I stroked my dong. I dipped it in her pure porcelain. I clutched her shapely butt in my large palms. I moved in. Changed position of my other hand so that I could gently touch her hot slippery sponge. She looked at my member all veins, doing its rounds diligently. I kept the vigil. Stroking and stroking until she cried out. Small spurts of moisture gushed out of her twat. I gently eased my hard penis outside and inside again. We made love, fucked and slammed. Changed positions and I was quite sure of my every move. I was erotically intoxicated, high. I fucked her like a gentleman. Letting her to come so many times until her pussy was making farting sounds. I gathered her closer. I gave her a series of tender small kisses to her pink tender lips. I eventually allowed defeat. I let go. I came in thick wads of hot sperm inside her. First two shots inside. She felt it hit her insides. She squirmed and moaned in pleasure. The rest I pulled out and let it hit her flat smooth stomach. She shuddered in ecstasy. I shook with my release and I collapsed on top of her. I felt on top of the world the rest of the day.

The next morning I became studious. I was attempting an essay question for my final term mark. The topic was leadership in nursing.

It was a tricky topic for me. I was not in management. I decided to look at my managers in my workplace and imagine what they face daily. Their experience became mine. I wrote the essay plan using that approach. Later I would ask Mei to check it for me. I yawned. I'd been at it since morning. It was 3 pm already. I reached for my hand phone and called Liong. I wanted him to bring one bottle. Study hard play hard. Later that day Leong came home with a bottle of absolute vodka. Mei played the flute. Wahoo! Yap, now we were serenading. After along while Vlarena and Leong darted into their room and got busy. I heard Vlarena's rapturous squealing. I shook my head turned to Mei and asked, 'where do they get so much energy to frolic and fuck?' we both laughed. Life was bliss at this time. I was living what I considered a normal life. I felt that this was the best way to live a full life. I was content. We tried to make life enjoyable by drinking whenever we could.

One weekend we were all at home. Mor came to see me at the apartment. I was busy attempting an essay question. When she entered I put it aside and turned to her. 'you study too hard Mbiramatako. Me I study three times a week only. It's enough.' Mor said. 'Yeah because it's a single subject, English. But me I have to do management communication and biology. Mor looked concerned, 'I understand. I recommend you take a break now. Maybe we go to the mall for a movie?' 'Ok good. I will ask the others if they want to join us.' I went to Mei s room and asked if she wanted to join me and Mor. She agreed and suggested after the movie we could buy something to eat. Leong and Vlarena came along. It was a splendid outing.

Mor finished her English course and went back to Korea. Her departure made me turn all my focus on Mei. Time flew for me. Mei became the uniting force for all of us. We were never in conflict. Mei had paternal instincts. She knew the common medicine to stock in the apartment. We never suffered uncontrolled colds. There was a remedy available in the house. She made sure the house was clean. She bought the washing soap every month and she didn't want money from us.

Going to work at the same time trying to study is a hard act. The hospital was short staffed. I was put on 12 hour duty. My degree programme required me to submit an essay every semester. Each semester was four months. I had homework every day. Drinking and my obsession with Mei did not make things easier.

The following weekend Leong, Vlarena and Mei called me at the Mall where I did my locum. They were home waiting for me. They'd cooked Chinese food. I reached and opened the door with my key. I went inside. I found them in the lounge. 'Guys I'm home!' I shouted. I put the bottle on the table. I served them myself. When everyone had a drink in hand I raised my glass. I said 'to bizarre and exciting times cheers!' and downed my shot. 'Cheers' they replied in unison. All drained their shots. Mei suggested that whenever we were free we must dance as a way to relax. She volunteered to play the flute. We followed her nimble feet as she played a soulful flute. Mei danced light on her small elegant toes.

I was off for three days. It was a good time to do final preps for my essay. The essay was due on the third day of my off. I needed to work hard. I was grappling with the conclusion. I knew I wasn't allowed to introduce new ideas there. So what should I include? Summarise only? I scratched my head. The door opened. Mei entered. She was formally dressed in grey slacks and white blouse. She had knocked off from the private hospital where she volunteered. She gave her work for free. The hospital looked after the disadvantaged. It belonged to a local Christian church. 'Hi Mbiramatako' Mei greeted. 'Mei, how are you? You look gorgeous no need to answer. I'm having a problem with my essay. Can you help me later on? When you are free?' 'Of course I always help you!' Mei replied as she kicked off her shoes and started unbuttoning her blouse tiptoeing to her room. My eyes were wide open. Why did she go? I thought to myself. I opened my textbook and read. I read for ten minutes but I couldn't remember anything. I went into the kitchen to look for a snack.

There were secrets being kept from each other. I had my own secret natural garden of marijuana in my room. My room was spacious enough to contain an in built cupboard made of louvers to allow air. I had a healthy plant of this mysterious herb. No one knew about it except me. Mei had smoked spliff before. Vlarena had never smoked. She didn't know Leong smoked. She discovered the other day when I rolled. This morning I watered my plant. And let the sun in. I lie in bed and read my book. The door opened. Mei stood inside the room. Her eyes were on the plant. 'This is not a flower Mbiramatako. You are growing drugs!' 'Its not drugs, it's a plant. I didn't want you to see this. I knew you wouldn't understand. Why didn't you knock? I told you already its good manners to knock first before entering. Look at you. Are you sure you couldn't find slacks to put on?' I admonished her. 'No need my shirt is big. It's covering down. Can you see anything?' Mei asked and swung around innocently. 'Never mind but you should knock before entering.' 'Why do you like to smoke weed?' Mei evaded my words. 'It makes me feel high.' I replied her. Mei sat at the edge of my bed. She gazed at me. 'I used weed for art to get into certain meditative mood. But I do not advocate taking it too much.' There was a soft knock and Vlarena entered. 'What is that bush. I think I know it.' 'It's a flower, a magical flower.' I corrected her. 'Mbiramatako why do you smoke it? Can I try? I want to taste the feel.' Vlarena flashed white teeth smiling. I took out my stash and rolled a joint. I lighted and passed to Mei. She dragged and gave to Vlarena. Vlarena coughed with the first attempt. I gave her a cup of cool water. She gulped. She gave me back the joint. She took it again. This time she smoked it successfully. We became very quiet. Suddenly Vlarena started talking but stopped mid way. She had forgotten what she wanted to say. I knew she was high already. 'How do you feel Vlarena?' Mei was concerned. 'I'm ok I don't feel anything. I want to eat something' Vlarena darted out of the room. She came back with a piece of cheese cake. She shared it with us. She didn't finish hers. She laughed unprovoked. She liked the experience. From that day we all smoked freely together. The next day I made sure to mention to Mei and Vlarena about the previous housemate. He used to smoke weed inside his room. I didn't know. He put a towel under the door. One night he came out of his room screaming. I came out and saw him spitting all over the place. He was shivering. After he calmed down I talked to him. He showed immense fear. His eyes wide open. I took him inside his room. I asked him what was wrong. He said he had been spiked and someone was controlling his brain. That someone knew what he wanted to do before he did it. I saw the weed! I took him for a walk downstairs. I met the guards and they told me that he was seen wandering around late at night for the past week. Vlarena's huge eyes were wide open. Mei was concerned. She told Vlarena 'Weed certainly sets us on a meditative tip. Those who do not know will feel strange and try to fight the feeling. That is a nasty experience. Do not smoke it if it feels like that. For those who can tolerate it and they put it to good use its very beneficial in opening the eyes.'

I continued with my tale. When I was young we had a tenant who was called Roger. He used to smoke weed. One day he smoked it inside his rented room. Outside some women hibernated in the morning sun. Some were washing dishes. The bathroom was communal outside near all this activity. Roger finished smoking and went to the bathroom to take a shower. He took off his clothes opened the shower and let the water hit him. He reached for soap. It was finished. He quickly thought of taking the new bar in his room. He opened the door and walked to his room, took the soap and was about to turn back. He saw his reflection in the wardrobe mirror. He was stark naked. 'No wonder the women had become deathly quiet and avoided his eyes when he came out of the bathroom!'

They'd not told me that Mei was lesbian. I didn't know much about my friends' background. They didn't know much about me. There was real trust. I bumped into Pathma my Indian friend. He was a former civil servant retired. Today he was grumpy. He said 'ayah, these cows are forcing me to take a bath so early in the morning.' 'Tell them to chill' I said. We both laughed. He cleared his throat. Gave a broad toothy smile and leaned closer 'I see you have one fresh cow to slaughter, have you slaughtered it already?' I knew what he meant.

I told him I was still busy trying. Slaughter day was imminent. We both laughed. I proceeded to my apartment. Pathma was not alone in thinking like that. Many who saw me with Mei, had a naughty gleam in their eye. It was obvious they thought we were banging.

At first I was timid in my advances to Mei. She was inviting. I got bold and pursued. She gave all sorts of excuses. She said she never had sex with a man. She didn't intend to start then. I formally proposed on one knee. I was rejected. I accused her of discriminating against me. I was a nurse and she a qualified doctor. She just laughed that aside. When my persistence became too much, she said to me, 'you pursue what is useless to you, instead of seeking something that gives life' 'are you some sort of a prophet, or angel?' I asked her. 'No I'm just me.' She looked at me and held my gaze. 'Everyone is what they are, my dear Mei' I returned her gaze. She changed the topic by asking something I didn't expect. She said 'Mbiramatako, I have a confession, every time I dance with you I feel highly aroused, very attracted. I get wet every time we do our little mask dance.' I thought, 'yes she is going to let me taste the fruit. if like that then ok.' She astonished me by saying 'I want to do a nude painting of you. I want to release all the sexual energy aroused by your presence. I want to paint you with so much passion the spirit of Mbiramatako shall be unleashed in that painting.' I looked at her in horror. I burst out laughing, 'are you serious? Well not me. I'm not going to pose nude for anyone.'

Adult education is tricky. I learnt that it's possible to have fun and still pass exams. The most important was balancing. It was easier to relax than study. Mei told me not to be so tight assed about study. 'Take it easy and follow your instincts to gain knowledge and you will find study easier for you.' Mei advised me. Mei proposed to buy ingredients for a marvellous dinner. We went to the local mall. As we approached the entrance, I saw a sudden flurry of activity. Three policemen were apprehending two nude women. The women struggled and shouted. We went closer. I noticed other young women and men with placards. They were dressed. Their placards advocated for legalization of public nudity. One placard read, 'women continue to be raped with clothes on', another one read, 'to be nude is to be free.' We skirted the crowd and entered inside. We headed to the supermarket. 'Mbiramatako, would you like to move around naked?' Mei asked me. 'Well I wouldn't mind if everyone else was nude also.' I laughed. Mei pondered, 'actually I have a friend who owns a private naturist resort in Chiang Mai. Maybe one day we plan and make a trip there?' I was incredulous 'that will be wonderful if it's for real.' Mei smiled. She looked at me and hit me lightly on my shoulder. 'Well, wait and see, God willing.'

We bought fresh chicken, ready made chapatti and gravy. At home we prepared a sumptuous meal. We sat in a round circle. The food and the liquor were placed in the middle. We enjoyed. It was a lovely dinner. After the meal we continued with the bottle. Much later we were swimming in the throes of the merry waters. I suggested trying an acoustic with my mbira and Mei's flute. We tried it and it worked! Vlarena was really good at dancing and very energetic. She was the one who usually called everyone to the dance. She was an excellent dancer. Mei was graceful. She was a dancing orgasm eager for the cooking stick. She was not very energetic in her moves. She had graceful energy. It was intense and languid. When we danced and I edged closer to her I felt it. The delicious energy. Mei was as delicate as the flower polite but there was a dangerous fire that she concealed. Mei and Vlarena were the sensuous energy source that sparked some of the most outrageously erotic funny dancing. We got used to hanging out like this.

From the day Mei proposed to paint a nude of me it became a game of tit for tat. I wanted her love and attention. She wanted to paint me nude! It took us nowhere. I still had not slaughtered my fresh cow. I was obsessed. I hunted her relentlessly. She was deft like a fish she always slipped away. I devised a trick of disbelief in her virginity. I teased her that she was not a virgin being so street wise. She allowed me to try to poke my finger inside her sweet petals. My hands were sweaty and shaky. I couldn't help myself. 'Get hold of yourself Mbiramatako. One chance only' she said as she slowly parted her milky soft thighs. I sighed in exasperated shaky breath. I advanced towards the pouted pink petals covered by fluffy hair. They were dewy and eager for touch. I made contact. The petal jumped to attention. Some of the sweet dew remained on my finger. I was warmly received but as my finger tried to proceed it could not without me hurting her. There was a soft stubborn seal there. I started to rub her clitoris. She didn't stop me. I continued rubbing softly, gently but insistently putting pressure. The fire in her erupted and squirts of hot dew shot out of the centre of her fire. I thought this is it' and tried to push my finger inside but could not go further.

In the end she calmly told me to move over. She said, 'don't expect to get another sweet treat like this.' She put on her wispy tongs. She looked at me and said, 'maybe you need to go beat it.' She indicated the power of my desire evidently outlined within my shorts. It looked like a hidden cockerel bone in my shorts. I took a deep breath and went to the bathroom. I had lost the game. She awakened my sexual desire. She made me realise who I was. I was desire. Intent on devouring her up. I took advantage of a time we were dancing alone. My stick was too close to the centre of her fire. Hers was an aroused fire hot and damp. The sweet scent of arousal wafted into my nostrils. This drove me mad. Transformed me into a hungry drooling hyena. I strived to enter the forbidden tunnel. Tear and rupture that hot stew pot. For so long I was denied until it hurt my loins. I put a lot of power and plucked open her delicate thighs. She tried to stop me until her face was red. I was quite a big man. She was slight though tall. I was nearly there I could feel the heat of it. The heat of the moment made her to catch her breath. For a fraction I felt her yield open the legs. I took advantage and drove straight into Jupiter.

It was her trick. As I pushed forward she moved her body aside. She lifted her knee. Twerp! Went the collision between my balls and her kneecap bone. She made the knee dig in some more. I doubled with agony. I howled involuntarily. Vlarena and Leong rushed in to find me doubled up in pain. Panting on the pine tiled floor. That was another embarrassing encounter. I thought I would never face awkwardness again. 'The stupid moron tried to rape me, call the police!' Mei shouted to Leong as she gathered up her torn brief black panties. She covered her thighs. She had defeated me again. I came face to face with reality. I went through a formal process of regret. I was compelled me to examine myself. The game could become fatal. I needed to control my self.

CHAPTER 6

Self perception against reality. I get confused. She obsessed my mind. Was she a witch? She had defeated me and tamed me. Her sensuality instead of giving rage calms me down. When I sleep the strangest vivid dreams come to me. Sometimes three nights in a row. Different but all vivid. I feel I can touch her. In my dreams she comes disrobed. She takes me to a strange path. She straddles me as a man might straddle a horse. She whips and drives me at great speed to an unknown destination. I feel fear. I'm mesmerised by her power. Her compelling beauty!

I was uploading my photos on Tumblr. I picked out one and took the camera from the glass table. Stood up and strode to Mei's room. I wanted to show her the photo. As I reached her door I stopped. I heard the unmistakable sound of sex! The sound of sexual activity is a mystery. Even faint the human senses can quickly decipher it. I turned back and went and sat. I shouted to her, 'get off your lovely lazy ass and come here. I got something wonderful to show you.' No answer. I tried again and received the sound of silence. Silence led to curiosity, 'could she be sleeping?' I went again to her door and knocked softly. I peeped inside. I quickly ducked back my head. Too late. I had seen already. I wanted to move away. I remained rooted to the sport. I was breathing fast.

I peeped in again. This time I looked longer. Mei was lying on the pink satin covers of her bed. Her eyes were closed. She was on her back with her legs so wide open, it's no wonder she claimed to be a gymnast. She was rubbing her swollen moist delicate flower using her smooth slender finger. She held my Zebra mask loosely in the other hand. She looked like a child overpowered by sleep in the middle of play. She was peaceful, so sensuous. I reached for my camera and snap! It took a photo. She quickly opened her eyes, shouted 'you!' She rose from the bed. What happened after that was unprecedented. She flew straight at my throat. The impact knocked the breath out of me. I thought she would reach for the camera but instead punch, punch! Stinging small bony punches that had me bleeding from the nose and my forehead. 'You are killing me!' I shouted to her. 'I took my Hippocratic oath, I shall not kill, but I will surely certify your death Mbiramatako!'

She grabbed the camera. Took out the memory card and threw it in the dust bin. I went to the bathroom to wash my face. I came back she was on the phone in the lounge. I glanced quickly inside. I saw the blue memory chip in the dust bin. I bent over and quickly reached for it. Boom! At first I was not sure what had happened. I flew forward. My face missed the bin by a whisker. The boom was her foot kicking me hard in my backside. Apparently the impact had reached my balls. I could feel the deep breathtaking agony only ball hurt can give. I snatched the memory card rose and bolted out of the room. She tried to block me. I was faster. She gave chase till I was out into the balcony. I couldn't wait for a lift. I quickly ran down the stairs. I looked back and saw no one. 'Lord, she was a tigress!' Afraid of the tigress I stayed out. I went back after allowing time for her to cool down. I unlocked the door and went inside. The light was on. Mei was sitting with Leong and Vlarena. 'Hey!' I greeted them. They all answered and Vlarena said 'come join us we are just about to wrap up the party'. I excused my self first went and took a shower. I came back into the lounge and joined them. We finished the last of the Chivas together. 'Let's have one joint to find sleep.

Mbiramatako can you play one soulful tune of the mbira?' Vlarena asked. 'I don't want weed. I am intoxicated already'. Mei replied. I looked at Leong to find out his choice, 'well, I want weeed' he said softly. We all laughed.

I took my mbira from my room and started imitating a tune by Kris Kristofferson and Chiwoniso Maraire called 'The Circle, Song For Layla A Attar and Los Olivadios.' I could play this tune on my mbira the whole night! Leong took out the weed. He was about to roll but Mei said, 'let me have the pleasure' she reached and took it. She rolled a fine sexy joint. Everything she touched became artistic. Her art finished, she took the lighter. She came and knelt beside me clapped her hands as I had told her women in my culture do. This is a way to show respect to the husband when giving him water or food. She looked exotic. She gave me the joint and lighted it for me. I dragged. She didn't immediately go back to her seat. She sat by my feet, resting her head on my lap. She threw her soft luxurious mane of deep black hair all over me. I offered her the joint but she refused. I gave it to Vlarena. Later she went and sat down at her seat. Vlarena and Leong said in unison, 'goodnight'. 'Going to partake?' Mei asked. We all laughed. We knew that when the two of them took weed they would be ravenous. I glanced at Mei and said, 'Oh homely girl, do you know UB40?' she shook her head. 'Oh yap of course! You were not yet born when they rocked the world. I really want you to be my woman. The one I give everything. The one who will give me a gourd of fresh water. The one who will look after my mom, my cousins, my daughter back home. Marry me Mei. You'll be the mother of a great nation. I'm the spirit of Mbiramatako. Come to me woman. I'll take great care of your delicate strong heart. Accept me. You shall not want. Your cup shall always be filled to the fullest.' Mei laughed. 'Oh now you employ your poetic charms? I say to you,'

Take me not to the house of Marriage

A bona fide affection ask not for conjugality, it wows,
Real love garners bliss you forget about the vows
Exclusive of intentions, no planned ceremonies
Adulation contrived in manipulation shall not suffice,
Manipulate me not to the house of marriage,
An abode of sedentary drama show
Curtain raise house, that's the sweetest chow
Consortium before marriage, living in the future
Who will lead to the altar in the android age?

Mei's huge eyes were more opaque and glittered gently as she looked at me. She was incredibly sensuous. I heard the rhythm of her gently quickened breath. She put her slender soft hand on my muscular thigh. It felt hot, sending blood into dangerous territory. She said 'I'm sorry Mbiramatako if my ideas are not more contemporary. If you find marriage agreeable marry a nice girl and settle'. She stood up, slapped me lightly on my cheek and kissed the same spot lightly. She said goodnight. I replied, 'night.' I went to sleep. My heart was heavy like it was carved in stone. I made a rash decision. I was never going to marry.

It was the month of April. Graduation time! I had done it. My second convocation was held at a different venue. The gowns and caps were a different colour. I booked my gown and cap at the university. Mei drove me to the Conference Centre building for the function. Vlarena and Leong came along. We went through the prepared motions of the programme. I received my certificate and photos flashed. I was the proud holder of a Degree (Hons) in Nursing Sciences. Outside I took more photos with Mei, Leong and Vlarena. Later Mei took us out for dinner all expenses paid.

The next afternoon I came back from the mall with groceries. Mei had just arrived from the hospital she volunteered. I brought her red wine and mozzarella cheese. She quickly grilled tender chicken to goodness. She was the perfect cook. I loved her cooking with all my heart. She only, knew how to make every other meal the way she made it. She had on a crispy white apron on top of a sleeveless tee and short mini skirt. She put the meal on the table. I brought the red wine and poured. We settled and enjoyed the sumptuous meal. Mei sat directly in front of me. We talked about many things before our conversation turned to religion. I wondered about her. Where did she stand with God? She was lying back into the sofa. She smoked the thin white Virginia cigarette she liked. Mei was an occasional smoker. Her brief skirt had moved high. I could see her tiny lacy thing. The mound was full. She looked at me through the smoky room. She was most sexy now. She was relaxed. I too. I was tamed. I learnt to enjoy rich experiences in peace.

The room was cool and dark. It was raining outside. The cigarette smoke made the room take an unreal hue. I asked Mei, 'what's your view about religion?' She replied as she puffed smoke rings out, 'do you remember that day I asked if you were coming from worship and you said yes? How come you were an eager beaver for my pussy? The teaching of your religion says no? People are more concerned with putting up a show than being really pious. Daily people bombard even on facebook. Am going to heaven! Am Jesus freak! Meet you at worship. Wake up brother! Hush, Mbiramatako. Stop talking for awhile. Stop grinning all over the place. Learn to shut up your brain. Your mouth to stop talking. Do you realise that silent and listen share exactly the same letters? Balance it out. Listen to your real self. You may discover a stunning revelation.'

I glared at her; she had touched a raw nerve. I countered, 'be careful pretty young lady! So much confidence and belligerence is the devil straddling you. I hope you retract your insults, even scientists like you have to respect someone's religion. I have deep respect for other religions. I'm willing to learn from them whenever I get a chance. If all of us become as rude as you and we all insult each other, soon there would be war and chaos. If you have anything to teach me stick to the facts of the lesson. Don't start by negative criticism and outright insults. Everyone needs to have religion, it's in born in us that every living being shall worship the Lord. A man without religion is like a man without soul, just existing. My religion is based on the living God.' Mei considered my words before she said 'I respect every religion. I'm sorry my words were hard. Most important is for us to have mutual respect. Agree to disagree and carry on in peace. Enjoy each other's friendship. After all true love does not discriminate between people.'

Later Mei said she wanted to go to her aunt's house to collect some flowers. She wanted us to go together. Her aunt and uncle's place was not far. We reached the house. Her uncle was sitting in the veranda. He rose and warmly received us. He kissed Mei lightly on the cheek. He shook my hand firmly. We all sat down in the veranda. Mei made introductions. Mei's aunt came and we greeted. She went inside. I heard the clutter of fine chinaware. I suspected tea. I hoped it would be green tea. She brought a hot pot of green tea. My favourite I thought to myself. I felt good. We settled down. Mei's uncle seemed unsettled but he looked alright to me. Suddenly Mei's uncle shouted, 'negro!' I was startled. I looked at Mei but she looked away. 'Bollocks! You so gay!' before I comprehend, spit! Straight in my face! My boiling mind thought that the old man's sense of humour was awkward and dangerous. Without further thought I rose. I swiftly lifted the old man by the scruff of his collar. He was very light. His expression showed genuine regret. I put him down and turned to Mei's aunty. I said sorry and strode to the car.

When we reached home I went straight to my room and lay down. Mei went to her room. Later I heard the shower running. She was bathing. I decided to shower too. After the shower I felt greatly refreshed. I still felt tense. I sat down in the lounge and read the newspaper. Mei came in still in her bath robe. She told me that Leong and Vlarena wanted us to meet at the pub later that night. I said quietly, 'ok can.' She sat beside me. She played her flute. She did not smell of perfume. She smelt fresh and clean. After a while she stopped playing. She ran her hand along my biceps. 'You are very angry. I am sorry I didn't tell you my uncle has got 'Tourette syndrome.' I looked at her in disbelief. I felt so embarrassed. 'You are a nurse so I thought you would recognise it. Instead you almost beat the shit out of my uncle! What are people learning nowadays in colleges and universities?' Mei stood up. She asked me 'have you ever been spanked?' she did not wait for my reply. She continued, 'spanking removes tension, pain is pleasure, come, we try.'

She led me to her room and made me lie in her bed. She took out a leather whip. She talked to me. She told me to take off all my clothes. I was hesitant but I relented. My member was restless. She instructed me to ignore it. I lay face downwards my cheek flat on the pillow. She still talked to me. Suddenly a sharp sting. I caught my breath. Before I could utter any word she whipped me twice in succession. I was swept away. She kept at it for a good three minutes. Stopped and threw away the small whip. She used her bare palm. The contact was electric. She kept at it for a long while. I lost count, maybe twenty minutes. I gasped and squirmed. I shot out hot sperm. She helped me to clean up. She whispered in my ear, 'you have just lived in the moment. That was you right there!' I went out to shower again. I felt light, I was floating. I felt strangely free and energetic. I was ready to hit the pub!

Saturday morning. Mei was in the kitchen, frying eggs. She's in a short jeans mini skirt and t shirt. I wasn't sure but it looked like she had nothing on underneath that mini skirt. The rump looked free under the skirt. My blood rushed south. I quickly switched off that energy surge. She brought the eggs, bread and some black coffee. Leong and Vlarena joined us. I helped to serve the food. We ate in silence. Vlarena and Leong groped under the table. Breakfast over I sat with Mei at the balcony. Vlarena and Leong went inside their room. I glanced at Mei, we both smiled. We knew what they were probably doing right now. Mei showed me her laptop. 'Do you know that in the northern coast of Colombia people actually enjoy sex with donkeys?' I laughed but sure enough there was the video with the young man caressing and cajoling a female donkey. Just as human males do when they are about to have intercourse with a human female. The young man patted the donkey and put his head on it. It is tradition in that particular Colombian village. I looked at Mei. I shook my head. Mei rose into standing position. I could see her nipples dark and rock hard through her white light t shirt. 'Let's go to my room where I can relax, I want to lie on my bed.' Mei said.

We rushed into her room. I sat on the settee. She lay on her bed. I confirmed my suspicions. She was not wearing anything underneath her mini skirt. Suddenly it was very hot in her room, though the aircon was on. She didn't seem aware of anything happening in the room. She said 'Have you ever heard of the sadhu aghori baba of India?' 'No' I answered. She continued, 'to become an aghori you have to meditate for twelve years non stop. The aghori stay at the coast where bodies are cremated. Every aghori must have a skull from which he eats and drinks. An aghori can eat anything from animal shit; food from bins and some aghori walk around naked. Some are reported to eat human flesh. They claim that if you reach the highest understanding of life, you won't cling to material things and life is every where and the same, so you must not discriminate, love all including the rotten and smelly. They can drink lavishly. They disown relatives and roam everywhere. They know they will always find a graveyard to stay.' I was aghast with horror. 'They sound like mad men Mei' I intoned. 'Yes, when you get out of your mind, you discover peace and simplicity. Your world is eradicated of fear. You can live at the grave yard it wouldn't matter.

In Papua New Guinea, some tribes still practice cannibalism. If we take our own modern values and impose them on their societies. We will jail these people for their own culture and beliefs. If the cannibalism that those tribes practice was chaotic rampant, wouldn't they have eaten each other up? There would be no humans left in that part of the world. They practice their cannibalism according to their traditions, which is sustainable and accepted in their society.' She paused. Looked at me and proceeded 'I gave you these extreme practices by humans to show you that human are varied in their culture and beliefs. The only force that can reconcile and unite all of us without trying to change each other is love. We don't need to colonize nations and coach them on how to live. Or send a high tech army of GIs to save people from their own governments. Nature dictates that we all look and do different things but within a limit that allows life to go on. The secret is to love and try to understand why people behave the way they do. Awareness always brings love. To love is to accept another individual the way they are. The moment we try to change someone in the name of love it becomes manipulative. Love is lost right there.'

'Mbiramatako, what is life, why are we living? Is there any purpose to this life?' I cleared my throat. She had caught me. It's a question I asked myself regularly. I still didn't have an answer. Godmother asked my views several times. I could not answer her. How could this sexy, feisty beautiful fairy of a girl go philosophical? I'm distracted by her physical beauty. She carelessly conceals it. I shook my head and said, 'I believe that life is what the individual makes of it. With blessings from God we may take the right path and succeed in life. I want you to Imagine a perpetual school where there is no exam and no report card, only continuous learning until you convey into graduation but never come back to share the great wisdom.' Mei turned to me and said, 'I think that life is about discovering life. It's a lifelong adventure filled with adventure. We never know about the future. Rather we work towards the future. It's elusive, unattainable. Who has ever said that yes they have reached the future? I believe humans can easily become bored. Life's a mystery to keep us ticking. That is life!' I'm a medical doctor. I studied art with some highly spiritual people. I got exposed to a lot of different religious practices. Sometimes I was sent to different remote hospitals. I'm quite sure of certain aspects of life. I'm also not sure about this life. There is an interesting trio of old men who think they got it all about life. One of them is a personal friend of mine. He was my parents' friend. I studied art under his tutorship. He is quite happy to host me at his naturist resort in Chiang Mai. I already called him. Do you remember I promised you that I would arrange for a trip to a naturist resort? We are going to Chiang Mai next week!'

During the course of the week we made preparations. Leong and Vlarena joined us. We flew to Thailand on a Thursday. Four hours journey. We arrived in good spirits. We connected via Air Asia to Chiang Mai. We hired a car at the airport. Leong drove us to the resort. Mei directed him. She was at the resort a few months before. She did her art tutorship there. It was a private property. Guests to the resort were mostly the owner's friends and business colleagues. Soon we arrived at the property. I saw cabins peeping through thick vegetation. It looked tranquil and uninhabited. Chiang Mai is located in a valley surrounded by hills and mountains. Alex's land was located around a mountain. It sloped down into a lush green valley. There was a river that ran through the property. The place was so serene I instantly felt at peace. The din of the city was left behind. Sounds of Birds chirping and cooing dominated the place. Distant sound of water flowing in the river pervaded the area. I was reminded of grandma Chihwiza's farm.

Alex came to the porch to meet us. He was white haired, elderly and majestic. He greeted us and led us in. We sat down and Mei said, 'how are you Alex?' 'I'm very well, thank you. I see you have brought your friends. That is good.' We smiled. Mei introduced us. She ended by saying 'and that is Vlarena my young sister.' Alex held Vlarena's small hand and enthused. 'You have grown young lady. It's good to see you. If I met you somewhere I wouldn't have recognised you.' I turned to Alex and commented 'this is a sublime place you have here. It's wonderful' Alex smiled and said, 'thanks, you are all welcome here. This is a naturist place. I made this place to find my spiritual being. To be at peace within this world. I'm quite sure that after staying here you will feel different. Beyond this arrival house there are your cabins. They are made from bamboo and very comfortable. The river is just nearby the cabins. It's good that you have come in the month of May. Its summer so you'll enjoy. This whole area is free to you.

Most of the other people that you meet will be nude. Don't freak out. You don't need to be nude if you don't want to. Relax and let everyone do as they please.' I cleared my throat and asked him, 'if you allow people to be dressed and some undressed, doesn't that create chaos?' Alex shook his silver locks of hair and said 'shy newcomers can keep their clothes on and mix well. Soon they'll feel out of place because they'll be outnumbered. They'll try and find out there is nothing to fear! Fear is as realistic as illusion. You can go to your cabins. Take a shower, refresh and meet me at my cabin for dinner.' We thanked him and went out.

The way to the cabins was a nicely manicured footpath. All around us were swaths of unkempt ground. An intense fusion of trees, grass and shrubs made the place mysterious. It was unkempt at the same time naturally orderly. There was a calming tantalising smell of wild flowers mixed with the smell of burnt cedars and burnt grain. Green foliage made it hard to see people from far away. At the curve of the footpath we met one man jogging. I noticed he was stark naked! We were all taken aback. The man continued. He waved to Alex and greeted in French. Alex answered in French. He looked at us and smiled. He said, 'don't say I didn't warn you.'

The cabin looked old and rough outside with grass and shrubs creeping near it. There was no 'nicely kept yard.' I felt edgy. I unlocked the door to the cabin and opened it. I gasped in delight. Inside the cabin was very comfortable. Nice furniture and spotlessly clean. It had three rooms inside and three small bathrooms inside. We shared the rooms. I went into my room. It was spacious and cool. A great relief from the outside heat. Cool and fresh from the shower I put on a fresh pair of shorts and tee shirt. I went out to the lounge room. Leong was there already. We waited for the ladies. Finally they came out and we filed to Alex's cabin. It looked more like a beautiful wooden house. It was big, spacious and airy fresh. Sturdy wooden beams supported it from the ground. We took off our shoes and climbed the short steps and entered inside. Alex was sitting cross legged on the floor. Facing him were two young beautiful women also sitting cross legged. Alex introduced them as his two wives. In between them were various silver bowels of steaming hot food. There was a variety of plates and silverware. We followed suit and sat around Alex and the two women. Everyone sat cross legged. I was in trouble. I tried but it was futile and painful. Every one laughed at me. Gosh, I remembered that grandma Chihwiza had urged me to sit cross legged back at her farm.

I used to sit cross legged. As I grew up in town we sat on the sofa. To put your feet up was taboo. In the end the taboo was that I sat with my legs out stretched in Mei's direction. She didn't mind. The food was delicious beyond words. It had character. It was cooked yet felt fresh to the fine senses of taste. It was fulfilling. Dinner finished Alex took us around the property. It was dark. The moon was full and bright. It lit the whole place in a warm luminous light. It felt magical walking in a group. We were attentive to the thin handsome frame of Alex as he showed us around. He talked to us in humorous wisdom. The property was surrounded by mountains and lush countryside. Alex explained that this region was known as Rose of the North. It was in existence since 1296 CE. It was once the capital of the ancient Lanna kingdom. 'Chiang Mai is within the Himalayan Mountains 700 km north of Bangkok.' Alex indicated. 'You tutored Mei in art?' I asked Alex by way of conversation. 'Yes, art is my life. I view the world in art. My other two friends are also artists though they hold other occupations. Art is how we met. Art also brought me together with one beautiful woman, Mei. I have an elaborate private gallery with some real great works. I will show you tomorrow.' Alex indicated the full moon, 'you see, when the moon is full the gravitational pull on earth is greater. The seas roll and rumble pulled by moon's gravity. Dogs howl and schizoids become restless. That is curious about schizoids. They sometimes have the most beautiful genius of mind. They are so sensitive that they feel the gravitational pull of the moon while we don't.'

'I remember this doctor, Carl Jung who was amazed when a schizoid told him the sun was the source of wind. Four years later he saw the same info published in a scientific journal. I believe what that doctor observed is that the psych is not confined to time and space. Dreams for example give a glimpse of this. Part of the psych is not dependent upon the confinements of this earth and human life.' Alex turned directly to me, 'The psych is not obligated to live in time and space alone. Don't you think Mbiramatako, that this may signify the continuance of life?' Life was a mystery to me. I was not sure what to say. Alex continued to talk as he led us back to his cabin. We sat at the porch. Most sat like Alex, cross legged, on the floor. I chose to sit in the huge swing inside the porch. It was big and comfortable. It could easily sit six persons of average weight. Mei joined me and cross legged on the swing. The young beautiful woman brought a tray with drinks and glasses. There was liquor in a glass bowel. She put it on the table. She poured and passed the small glasses of liquor around.

Alex took one shot and put the empty glass down. I followed suit. The liquor was surprisingly smooth. So light it felt like it was vaporising as it went down my throat. Its searing curious heat rushed down to the belly. An immediate warm glow rose from the pit of the stomach to the brain and all over my body. It was the most wondrous high. Higher and higher it snapped me into another world. It was delicious. I looked around me. I could see every one looking back at me sheepishly happy. Alex remained tranquil with a happy twinkle in his eye. We looked at each other again. We all burst out laughing. We tried to control and compose our selves. It was in vain. We laughed until it hurt. Tears streamed down our faces. Mei lay on my lap and tried to control it. Later we were able to contain the laughter. 'Alex, what brand of liquor is that?' I asked. 'It has no brand. I brew it myself. It is the finest liquor you will ever taste in your life. It's matured. The oldest like the one we took now is twenty plus years special reserve.' I had a special reserve of a satisfying sleep that night. Early next day I was awoken by the birds chirping. It was five morning.

I took a shower and went into the lounge. I heated some water, made a cup of coffee, sat and enjoyed. The others joined me shortly after. They took cups of coffee. We went out to Alex's cabin. He sat on the porch, fresh as the morning air. 'Good morning' we hummed. He greeted us back. He asked if we wanted breakfast. It was too early. Plus we just had coffee. 'Ok then' he clapped his hands together. He announced for us to go to the river right away and enjoy fresh nature. We took fishing rods. 'Today everyone gets to catch their dinner' Alex shouted as he led to the river.

CHAPTER 7

A cool fresh breeze wafted gently. It amazed me in its power to sway the branches of the huge trees around us. The sweet smell of humid humus and vegetation lingered faintly in the air. Everywhere I looked I could see masses of flora and fauna. Trees twisted with lichen and moss. Bamboo trees everywhere. A number of people were walking from their respective cabins. Some cycling, some jogging and others were fishing by the river. They were all nude and waved to us in good spirit. Alex did not comment anything. I felt discomfort. Not at their naked state but at our own clothed state. We were the only people dressed. It felt awkward. We proceeded to a spot Alex chose. He was talking to us as we went about fishing. 'You said your full name is Kant Mbiramatako. Do you know a great philosopher called Immanuel Kant?' I replied that I did not know him. Alex continued, 'he came up with a theory that humans have prior knowledge in them and knowledge gained from experience. Kant argues that our mental faculties shape our experience.'

The sun had risen high and hot. It was 11 am. Insects were alive with the heat. They jostled for the sweetest nectar from the water lilies spread out like a pink and green carpet by the rive banks. Alex had caught his fish. The rest of us caught also. I caught three big cat fish. We were all feeling very hot. Other people took a dip into the river to cool down. I felt hot. The cool river water was very tempting. 'Mei lets take a dip' I suggested. Mei replied that we had not brought a change of clothes. I asked that we dive naked but she was reluctant. All of us were not comfortable to take off our clothes. Alex reassured, 'do not worry everyone you see is a special guest. Their attention and goals are to find as much spiritual happiness as possible. No one notices each other's nudity.' It was hard for us to undress in front of the crowd. In the end no one took a swim. We went back to Alex's cabin to have brunch. Alex promised to take us up the mountain around 5pm. He advised us to eat well and rest well. It was taxing to climb the mountain.

At five we all trailed behind Alex going up the mountain. We met a few other people all nude doing various sunset activities. Some were exercising by stretching. Others jogged up the mountain. I saw one tall European woman jogging; she was topless but had bikinis on. She smiled and waved at us as she passed. As we reached the summit I was startled to see one man dressed in clothes normally dressed by Buddhists. He was in the lotus position balanced precariously on an outcrop of rock. The rock extended outwards towards dangerous slops. Alex explained that the man was meditating. We didn't disturb him. We only disturbed the grass, shrubs and the birds that took immediate flight in fright at our invasion of their natural habitat. We foraged around. Alex showed us a variety of natural species. There were mushrooms which he claimed gave psychedelic experiences. He offered me to try. I refused. No one offered to try. We proceeded. Alex explained that some plants were holy because God intends them for man to use wisely in order to gain wisdom. Some humans abuse the power of the natural herbs. Hence authorities made them illegal to protect the people. 'Do you know the peyote? It is sacred to the Native Americans and is protected by law. Natives can use it for their spiritual purposes. Non natives caught with it will be arrested. Man made drugs like LSD can also alter consciousness. You go on a trip. Personally I prefer natural herbs rather than man made.'

We found a good spot to sit and relax. We were out of breath except Alex. The mountain looked small but it was quite a task to climb. Climb any mountain. The reward for pain becomes pleasure as the majestic view of the land below the mountain comes to view. That mountain straddling Alex's property enabled us to see the full majesty of the temples of Chiang Mai. From this vantage point we saw the city outlined in our view. We saw many temples, small houses and shops. Alex pointed out more than 30 temples dating back to the founding of the principality. They were in a combination of Burmese, Sri Lankan and Lanna Thai styles. We l relaxed facing the valley below. Alex asked if we had any questions, even general knowledge ones. He was a wonderful fountain of knowledge. I looked at him and asked 'what colour is the polar bear's fur?' Alex replied, 'the fur of the bear is transparent and hollow. It reflects the colour of the snow and looks white.'

We were all silent for a while. During that moment of silence we heard the sweet sounds of nature. The dove cooed, the trees whistled and the river quietly splashed in the distance. I opened my mouth to speak. Alex signalled me to silence. The sounds of nature serenaded us. Alex pointed to a bush and whistled. We looked in the direction he was looking. Behold a huge white cobra, its eyes red. 'It's high on the weed. It's been eating the bush of the weed. The weed looks good and well matured. The cobra chose the best herb' Alex chuckled. The cobra slithered away into the bushes and disappeared. 'Why didn't he attack us?' I asked. 'Only humans are aggressive without purpose. No animal will attack you unless its hungry or you attack it. Or you are a threat to it. Go and pick up that gold so we can all share the natural goodness.' Alex indicated to me. I stood up uncertainly. I wasn't sure if the cobra had gone. Mei stood and said 'I will go with you. I also want to harvest.' We chose the most lively looking buds and leaves. We gave some buds to Alex. I gave some to Leong and Vlarena. Leong took out a packet of rolling paper and threw it to me. Alex took out his pipe. He stacked it up with the natural herb. Mei asked him why she had felt strange when we were all silent. We all agreed feeling a bit weird. Alex said 'what do you think? I don't know also, maybe it was your consciousness coming to light' he concluded as he lit his pipe. We were still rolling our joints. 'Whilst you are rolling and before you smoke that stuff I want to tell you an interesting short story. I learnt this story from one of the greatest philosophers of all time, according to my view, of course. His name is Alan Watts. I will tell it as how I understood it.'

'Leong tell me what is voluntary and what is involuntary when we walk?' Alex asked. Leong looked lost. He scratched his head. I was not sure either. I kept quiet. Mei tried, 'when we feel that we are the ones deciding to walk we must ask ourselves how we decide, isn't it.' She was silent. Not sure how to continue. Alex took over. 'Do we first decide to decide to walk and stand? We don't, usually we just decide the destination and we walk there. Look at us breathing right now. Everyone here can feel that we breathe intentionally. When we don't think about breathing as in someone for example, in a coma in hospital without breathing aid machines, breathing still goes on. Is it voluntary or involuntary? It's involuntary yeah but who decides it to be involuntary if say you are in a coma?' Alex looked at each of us.

We were halfway through with our joints. We were buzzing high. The weed was extremely strong. I kept control. I looked at the others. I guess they felt the same. It was quite a sensuous circle. Mei and Vlaren were wearing low waist jeans in accordance with trend. The exposed rear to the point of the rim was very alluring. It was innocently sexy. It was hard to concentrate on Alex. He kept on talking. He kept us attentive. 'Most of us believe that the mind manipulates the body into various actions. The reality is that the body manoeuvres and manipulate itself utilising the mind. The brain needs the body to work perfectly. Same like how the brain needs and use electronic aids like computers or calculators to aid it in its function. Humans should be whole and not feel like separate entities in one human. If we separate ourselves we became divided into half man. We start to look at life in terms of us possessing a body when we should feel like a body. We feel that we have a natural tendency to live and to make love to each other instead of experiencing and enjoying love.' Alex puffed on his pipe. He looked at us. 'The involuntary can be synonymous with God breathing in us as he does all the time, only we are not aware of it', said Vlarena. Alex quickly agreed 'Very good, the omnipotent God.' Mei turned. She looked at me her eyes huge with wonder, 'so omnipotence is manifest in me, oh my God.' She screamed. We were wide eyed. The high of the weed momentarily forgotten.

We were attentive. Staring at Alex. Daring him to go on. 'Omnipotence is that which does action without know how or experience. We all perform some actions as organism without us being aware of actively making the decisions to do so.' 'Could this be the same as Immanuel Kant's critique of reason theory?' I asked. 'Could be yes' agreed Alex. He continued, 'all of us are unconsciously performing all the various activities of our organism or being. This could also be referred to as super awareness to qualify its real significance. You see how all humans worship in one form or another, who taught them to worship? So consciousness or awareness is when we allow ourselves into that which performs certain activities for us, it actually evolves into a unique happening or phenomena of awareness.' Alex paused and smiled. He looked at us and proceeded 'When you look around this mountain, you are conscious of as much as you can notice, you see an enormous number of things which you do not notice. For example, I look at that Frangipani tree here and somebody asks me later weather it was fully flowered or not? I may not know fully flowered, although I've seen the flowers, because I didn't attend to that detail. But I saw all the details, in other words I was aware but only I didn't register and pay attention to it. Do you all understand? And per chance I could go under hypnosis where I would get my conscious attention out of the way I could recall the full glory of the fully flowered Frangipani tree!'

'The great philosopher Alan Watts argues that humans don't have a separate dual entity, that is the physical and spiritual but that it's like a process, a pattern, a dance of energy that manifest into individual you and me. Have you ever looked at life this way, that the eye is where light originate from. Without eyes the sun would be heat but not light. We elicit light out of the universe. It's our eardrums that process sound from the air, which is why deaf people, cannot hear what those who have the ability to hear can hear, no matter how much they try to listen. All organisms on this earth turn the universe to life.' My mind was racing. I said. 'Life is how we see it.' Mei added 'there is a disorder we met in the medical field, where the person who has stroke insists that he has not stroked. The condition is called anosognosia. Sometimes anosognosia happens in patients who become blind. They won't admit it and will remain adamant even if you prove to them that they are blind.' Mei continued 'people in that situation see the world as per their medical conditions but they don't know it. They see the world differently from us. Their world is different from us.' The mosquitoes were hungry and eager to feed as dusk turned to early nightfall. Alex smiled 'its getting dark lets go back down.' As we descended we were all quiet. Deep in thought. The bull frogs down the river were croaking. Crickets were squealing continuously. An owl swooped down on an unfortunate mouse. It flew up and perched on our cabin's roof. Alex turned to me. He told me that he heard some societies associate the owl with witchcraft but it was innocent. 'It was associated with witches because it is nocturnal. It perched on people's houses looking for rats. That convinced people it was doing something witchy up their roofs! You better get used to the bull frogs noise. Do you know that bullfrogs don't sleep?' Alex concluded by asking me. I shook my head. That night we decided to relax and let Mei play her flute. I was excited, I loved Mei's flute like fresh fruit. Mei took out her flute and Alex explained to me that the flute was called a Chinese bamboo flute. Mei added that her uncle, the one I almost throttled, the one with tourettes had given it to her. She was a teenage girl for her 17th birthday. Mei played sweeter than the Pied piper. Lucky there were no children around. Otherwise they would vanish with Mei's melody. I took out my mask, donned it. I swayed to the sweet music from the flute. It was the sweetest flute. Everyone loosened up and relaxed. Alex was impressed. He was interested in the zebra mask.

He took it and looked closely at it. 'It's original leather from a male bull. Very genuine, where did you get this?' he asked. I told him that my grandma Chihwiza gave it to me long ago. I was five years old at her farm. 'What original colour do you think was on this zebra? Did black colour come on it first then white colour or white colour came on it first?' Alex asked. 'Probably black, black is potent' I said. Alex shook his head and looked around at us. 'They came upon and formed the colour of the zebra together, simultaneously. They always happen together. On and off, together.' Mei indicated the mask 'Mbiramatako, you remember the first time I saw this I told you yin yang?' Alex agreed, 'one implies another, black implies white. White implies black same like I imply Mbiramatako and Mbiramatako imply me.' I jumped in, 'if it's like that then there is no you and me separately.' Alex nodded. He gestured, 'consider this, why is it that among humans the only difference in them is the image we see outside. The real nifty gritty of life is the same inside. We all breathe and have livers to detoxify. Why is it that the illegal organ trade is affecting people from third world countries? The rich want their organs. They identify themselves as separate from them, amazing isn't it?' Alex pondered. He had a strange look in his eye. 'Good night. Tomorrow I suggest we go for a walk in nature. Have a picnic, maybe a swim, ok?' We replied 'yes!' in excited tones. We felt like young kids again. We rushed out and went to sleep.

The next day we were all up by 5 am. We took our showers. Gulped down some coffee and rushed to Alex's cabin. Prepared food was already placed at the porch. Alex came out and smiled good morning. We all replied. We carried the food and followed Alex down the path. We admired the flowers, the beetles and occasional humans all nude. My senses, my nose was alive to various smells and sounds of a fresh morning. The morning air smelt dewy and damp. At the same time it was refreshing. The varied flora appeared in purples, maroons and light blue all swaying gently in the morning breeze. They were waving good morning. The big trees around sang good morning in whistles and whispers. Their branches and leaves moved to the morning breeze. The insects, the bees did not bother to whisper good morning. They were busy nibbling and sucking nectar from various flowers adorning around. I spotted a dung beetle that was involved in acrobatic feat on its front feet. The back feet pushing a huge ball of squirrel dung. We went near the river. Alex chose a picnic spot. The place was surrounded by thick bush. It provided a refreshing cool natural shade. We sat on rugs we had brought. The walk made us ravenous. We tucked into the food. It was splendid.

The meal finished we relaxed. Alex indicated the river, 'listen to the sound of the river.' We became silent. The song of the river became clear. A wistful harmonising presence. A flowing silent energy. We began to feel deliciously drowsy. We hit the brink of slumber. Alex arose and suggested everyone take a dip into the river. Today we went prepared with swimwear. We changed behind the bushes and dove into the water. The cool refreshment of the river water was exhilarating. Everyone played like kids in the water. We felt invigorated and alert. We relaxed. Alex said, 'if we really want to discover the nature of being, we do not necessarily need to put huge amounts of effort, just as we don't need to know how we work our liver to detoxify. Me, Mbiramatako, Leong or you Vlarena, we look so distinctly different but we are made up of the same material and intelligence inside ourselves. That is what connects us though we are separate individuals. We could say there is strong unity and consistent affinity between what happens on inside you and what goes on outside of you. Neither the inside nor the outside is stronger. They form one entity. What Mbiramatako or Mei does is what the whole creation or cosmos does and what the cosmos does is also what we all do. Not you or I in the meaning of our artificial self importance or esteem also called the ego. It is a small proportion of our awareness. The real we, are the sense of the sum of the psychopathic body or organism, aware as well as unaware.' Alex stopped for a while. He responded to a wave from one of the nude guests.

He lit his pipe and continued, 'so what is life? What is the meaning of life?' Alex glanced at us one by one. 'Is life about making money, becoming rich, sex on the beach, marriage, raise family, retire and kick the bucket to heaven knows where? There is a lot to life to hang on for a while for. Actually there is an infinite trait of magnitude of the world to which our faculties answer to without our deliberate awareness. Imagine vibrations such as cosmic rays which have wavelengths to which our faculties are not tuned and cannot decipher. There is still a lot that we can discover, wonder about and enjoy. We need to discover life one piece at a time. 'It's a process, a journey to enjoy. Humans' lack of knowledge of unconsidered circumstances which can arise into our awareness is the main reason of the self importance which in itself is not tangible, but just an idea. When we try to make sense of that 'idea', that is when we are tempted to say life is meaningless.' Alex pondered us and broke into a smile, 'we need to go and have lunch. Remind me to continue.'

We went back to the cabin. Lunch was laid out on the porch. We ate and rested for thirty minutes. We settled and listened to Alex. 'To begin with let's go for biology. We can look at Life as interplay of pulses or tremors with a particular arrangement of neurons also known as nerve cells. The pulses or vibrations produced by the sun become light and heat when they interplay and interact with a living organism. Have you ever considered that light beams are there but we cannot see them unless some particles like dust particle reflect it and the moon and stars, we only see them at night when the sun's light beams reflect on them, but they are always there. Take another example of the electric current, and how it needs the positive pole and the negative pole in a wire in order for electric current to flow. It always takes two for anything to happen. The cosmos has all the ingredients or makeup of life freely present everywhere, including the tide and phenomena of light, heat, weight, hardness, but it needs the living human and other organisms to bring it to life.' Alex smiled and said 'ok let's move around some, what you say?'

The next day Alex approached us looking pleased. He informed that his friend and business partner was coming to spend the weekend with us. 'His name is Eric. He is quite eccentric, as we all are. He's a lecturer at Bangkok University. He teaches psychology. He has a doctorate in human behaviour and psychology. You'll love him. He is a great chap.' On Saturday morning Eric arrived. He was tall with white hair and white beard. A handsome old man. Very strong. He kept an upright posture without putting effort. He was like a young man in an older well manicured well cut body. He was indeed eccentric. He came with his three wives, all young and sweet looking. There was an excited flurry when he arrived. He injected an electric energy at the resort. We all greeted and introduced ourselves. He told us his name and introduced his three wives. Of course he knew Mei. He went inside his allocated cabin with his wives. We were going to meet after breakfast and take a tour to the river together and swim.

We meant to view Alex's Art gallery earlier but had got busy. When Eric came Alex took that opportunity for all of us to take a tour of the gallery. After breakfast we hurried out and followed in single file to the gallery. Eric had come out natural and his three wives. I was trying my best to be polite but the eye always go where it's most forbidden. I noticed that Eric's wives had voluptuous breasts and big bums. Most women I met here were very beautiful but they had flat bums. Eric's three wives all had big buttocks. I asked Mei 'is it possible that regular sex makes someone look beautiful?' Mei shook her head. She didn't know. They were all normal about their nudity. Eric turned to me and laughed, 'Alex told me that you all are too shy to be natural, why the guilt? Is it the original Adam and Eve one?' he asked and we all laughed. 'You must liberate yourself from guilt.' The art gallery was a professional gallery. Adjacent it Alex indicated the art classroom. Presently he didn't have any pupils. He was half way through a project. We entered inside. Alex went through the works with us. I'm no professional in art. I followed his, Eric and Mei's comments about the various arts displayed. My attention however was caught when we reached Eric's collection of artworks. He showed with his immaculate hand. 'Ladies and gentlemen, my collection. 'The Butt.' Piece after piece of art of different beautiful buttocks of women adorned his collection. Different butt in all pose imaginable. It was weird, it was beautiful. 'I wouldn't mind staying there' I pointed to an art collection. 'That's Joe's work. The man works hard. The good people never get noticed. It's the killers that get headlines.' Alex reflected. Joseph's collection brought to life his dreams. Elaborate designs of sleek cities. It was an impressive idea. Sleek bridges connecting clean communities. Cities where we could live in peace and never have to worry about rent. Cities were we can take walks at any time of night without fear. He envisaged cities that every one lived equally. No classes according to riches. Class society fades in comparison with what I saw in his art. His ideas looked so sublime. 'Why is his government not supporting him?' I threw the question to Eric. 'Young man that is exactly what I want to know. That was great food for the eyes. We turned to nature by going down to the river to take a swim.

We reached the river and jumped in. A chaotic splash of water ensured. It was fun. Some decided to fish. Eric went with his fishing line to talk to a nude couple. They all knew each other here. The other people knew that Alex had guests. Often they would pass by our group and greet us. By day two at the resort we had became familiar with most people around the property. There was one lady, tall and beautiful. She was athletic. Most times we saw her jogging around the property topless. Always she kept her brief tongs on. That morning she came towards us. She greeted us talked to Alex and went on her way. Later we met her again at the river. Her perfect form lay on a big pink towel. She was applying sun lotion. She looked at me with a cry for help in her eye. I went and she turned on her stomach. I applied the oil for her. She was topless but as usual her tongs were on. She had very beautiful soft skin. She flashed me a smile and said thanks. I went and joined the others. At 11 pm we assembled at our usual picnic sport. Everyone was feeling happy and carefree. Eric was lying down with his head on the lap of one of his wives. He rose into sitting position, crossed his legs and accepted food offered by his wife. He munched. It was delicious food. We all enjoyed it. 'Shyness is like a barrier to development. Transformation of the individual is hindered. You must discard anything that inhibit the real you. Don't be addicted to anything, be it drugs, sex, power nicotine, anything. Be free to direct your life. Most humans have an already existing sense of fault or guilt. There are always people ready to fuel on that guilt and shame. Ordinary people, people in authority and clergy can be brilliant in making you feel guilty. You have to be alert always and watch what game people are playing.'

'Your behaviour shows me you still have doubts about your own self and sexuality. Confront it and you will be liberated. You will be able to enjoy life at a better level. Take sex for example, many people feel very guilty and shy to discuss about it. That is maybe good for society's morality. The individual must mature and discover own self sexually. All must learn to be responsible in that freedom. We must respect love, however we may define it. We must observe it and never reject it. It comes in different forms by different methods. Different people view and understand it differently. The idea of love should be continuously fostered. Falling in love is the same sort of thing as the mystical vision. A grace. In its light we see people in their divine aspect. Love is a mystical intoxication! Most religions adore God's beautiful gift of a companion to man, woman.' Eric reflected and planted a small kiss on his wife's pink lips. She flashed even white teeth and kissed him back. Her cheeks flushed pink rose. He continued, 'I understand that the Arabs have 'the perfumed garden, a tribute to the love of woman. The eastern religions have the karma sutra. In the Christian book of proverbs we are urged to enjoy our wives whilst they are still young.' 'In my culture, young man and women about to marry are taken for retreats and separately taught about sex. They are mentored on how to satisfy each other sexually. This is a traditional custom.' I added. 'So sex is essential and beautiful. As you have noted sex is mostly acknowledged in most societies. It's mostly valued for its reproductive use only. Any other sexual activity becomes sin.'

'I think this is what affects most of us. The guilty feeling about sex. Sex is a lot more. It is divine, an intense apocalypse of the celestial.' The flowers around us seemed to be in competition. Bursting into life and some tumbling down in decay and death. The insects were constant companions to the orchids and petunias. The willow birds chirped and eyed the insects. The eagle hovered above, its eye on the small birds. It was a busy dash for food and survival. The squirrel made a frantic run across from us. It careened the Rambutan tree. Moments later it sat on a branch nibbling at fresh juicy fruit. The unsavoury snail not to be outdone moved slowly in the decaying matter of vegetation. Leaving slime along its trail. This is life, its all happening at once!

I looked at Mei. She looked back at me. She quickly ran her tongue over her lips. She looked away. 'The erotic fucking and wriggling motion of an aroused male and an aroused female can be related to biology. Sex becomes a mirror of the most important play of the universe. Sex brings partners closer in united ecstasy. Sex is tantamount to an anointing, a sacrament, the production and physical sign act, an inner, spiritual grace bringing about love. Animals are not at humans' level in their sexual world. They do it for reproduction. Eric paused took a sip from his glass and said, 'I tell you what? Sexual biology regenerates and reverberates throughout the universe. It's a rapturous play.' Eric looked at us all. He smiled broadly. 'Preaching is moral violence. I will be quiet for now.'

I stood up and walked to the edge of the river. I took off my swimming trunk and dove into the water. I swam and swam far from our picnic place. I felt energy. When I swam back everyone was in the river playing with water and swimming. I joined them. We all came out and I saw that every one of us was nude. Finally we were in the nude. My brain was very active. I didn't want to look. It was forbidden in my conscience to see another naked body. Even my own naked body I seldom saw it in full naked glory. It was a challenge. My mind grappled with thoughts of guilt. If any of the females caught me looking at them what would they think of me? I think every one felt the same. There was momentary awkward silence. We could not look each other in the eye. We felt like we were all too close for each other's comfort. My skin tingled. From what I was not sure. Childhood feelings of shame and guilt flooded me. I was in confrontation with myself. It felt like the moment of reckoning. The experienced nudists were ok. They felt for us. That made them self conscious and unease. When we walked back the tension was broken. Moving about helped to let go of the moment and carry on. I felt more comfortable walking behind Mei, watching her generous buttocks wiggle freely. She turned and gave me a reprimanding look. I was enjoying myself. We filed back to the cabin. All of us in the nude. I walked right behind Mei, looking at the white shadow of bikinis against tan where the sun reaches. Her shapely figure inspired me to rhyme thus,

Miss May

Nevermore gaze afore such an adept silhouette
Lilliputian waist, a bounteous form to filch home
Enchanted I eternally recite Mei
I forever tingle to grasp a nice round butt,
I crave for close confabulation with butt, but I never
    waiver
Turn gross and coarse crude like a learner
I exalt flawless genesis, with it I hanker to flow naturally
Bare and dressed in audacious beauty, it feels so natural
To exist, to love

To exist in love and to walk close to Mei in wonderful nudity was the most natural feeling ever! We went to our respective cabins to bath. Alex had lit a small glowing fire in the porch of his cabin. The weather was warm but the fire was attractive. It was getting dark. The moon was peeping out from the horizon. We entered and sat on rugs. I went to the big swing. Mei followed suit. Eric came in and sat in the corner with his three wives flanking him. Alex sat in the middle of his two beautiful wives near the middle of the porch. Alex's beautiful wives were quiet. They were subtle in showing their affections to Alex. Sometimes I spied a furtive caress by one of the wife. At times one would brush away insects and mosquitoes from him. The way they both sat close to him showed strong affinity and bonding. They were blissful in their marriage.

We were all nude. God what an atmosphere! It was overwhelming and beautiful. All these human forms. Alex and his wives dished out portions of food and passed it around. More small bowels of delicacies followed before the famous liquor. This time it did not make us laugh. It made me feel warmth and relaxation. More relaxation and euphoric experience awaited us. Eric gave me a wooden case engraved in exotic drawings. I opened the lid. Inside was some quality marijuana. He said that he grew it himself at the resort when he was on his annual holiday. I took some and Mei took also. We rolled enough joints for everyone. Everyone lighted up. We enjoyed the rich herb. The naughty part of my mind wanted to sneak looks at all the naked women around me. The fact they were also looking back at me in nudity made it hard to stare. Alex's wives and all the other women talked among themselves the tricks of nudity and comfort for the woman. Later Mei told me that they taught each other how to sit with the heels of the feet protecting the female genitalia. No wonder when we sat I saw only the pubic mound. The real genitalia were cleverly hidden by the posture of sitting!

Eric had a sparkle in his eye as he looked at me. He inquired, 'do you and Mei have a little something going on? For I must swear I sense so much repressed energy entangling both of you. I don't feel that when I look at Leong and Vlarena!' Leong and Vlarena looked at me and Mei. They smiled. I smiled and looked at Mei. She looked away. Eric addressed the whole group, 'I tell you all this, eh, sex is the bomb. Imagine three bombs a day how much energy? I make love to all my three wives whenever we can. Sometimes I don't sleep at all. I always fuck thoroughly each of my three wives. I make every session fresh for each of my darlings. I don't stop shagging until she tells me that she has come and is satiated. Lilly especially is naughty. Eric turned and tinkled Lilly's delicate chin. 'She won't tell me she has come. Though I can feel from her pussy that she has come several times already, I continue to shag and shag. One day we shagged until it was so intense we both exploded in orgasmic bursts of light. We slept till the next morning. That was the only day I missed my duty to the other two. I told them to tell the truth if they come. If they don't tell me I won't stop shagging.' Shagging for living was Eric's style. He went on to say, 'I guess that is the only thing keeping me sane. To have a reason to cling to this life. Otherwise I could just let go and experience the final ecstasy. Oh life, what an alluring beautiful dash.'

'All of you get rid of any fears in your life including the greatest fear of all, death. Never perceive life as purposeless. When we see life as meaningless we are bound to be neurotic and shrinks will recommend social activities. I think the problem start when we feel that life must have a purpose and must be an ensign. At times we feel that life is more worth if we belong to a group in society. It could be church group, boozers club or political elite. We take being alone as loneliness. We cry if we find ourselves alone. It's possible to be alone and be in perfect peace! In this world it is very easy to feel that the world is a trap, it is a mechanism, its electronic and neurological mechanisms into which we just got caught in without choice. As humans we have to contend with a body that crumbles apart, that can be afflicted by horrible diseases like cancer, a body that can contract sexually transmitted diseases. Sometimes physicians can only help to mitigate the impact of disease but in most cases they will give up also. This may lead us to self immolate.'

'Is life really so bleary? Is this all that there is to life?' Eric turned to Alex. 'Let's have some more natural herb and a little bit of your golden merry waters. We call it quits and tomorrow at 5 am sharp we take a nude brisk walk to detoxify. Rid our bodies of these indulgencies we are enjoying right now.' That night we were young again. We groped our way to the cabins to sleep blissfully. Eric's cabin was next to mine. I heard grunting and moaning and ecstatic screams. I smiled. Eric was fulfilling his erotic covenant with his three pretty wives. I drifted off to sleep.

CHAPTER 8

The next day we walked down the lane. Eric explained about the lane, 'Alex, Joseph and I agreed to pave these paths without digging out the natural grass and roots or disturb the geology. We concentrated especially on taking out all rough objects and even out rough ground. We rehabilitated it for walks without shoes. We believe that when you are nude it must be from foot to head. No hat no shoes and everything else between. Yes celebrate life! You don't want to be beaten by a mere flea which can jump about 130 times its height, same as a person jumping the arch of St Louis! Come on people, jump around, jump around!' Eric urged us into warm up. 'Everyone take a huge deep breath.' We followed his instructions. 'No, no, no, stop every one, space out and stretch your arms out and far, yawn loudly, yawn.' We all followed and yawned. 'Ok I want every one to relax. Look up at me here in front of you. Ok breath, relax and follow the sound that I am going to make.' He proceeded to demonstrate. We followed and he kept repeating and we followed for about twenty continuous minutes then he said stop. We all felt strangely light headed. I felt outright high, the zing like I had just smoked weed. I looked at Mei and I said 'I feel my face feels funny' she laughed and replied that she felt strangely euphoric. It was clear we were all ready for the walk.

We walked at leisure until we reached a flat rock that stretched out. The spot overlooked the shimmering river in the near distant. Flowers burst out in glorious colours of orange and lilac. Bougainvillea in purple passion lured insects. The bees fought for the sweetest nectar of the blossoms of petunias in all shades of pink, white and purple. It was a buzz. We put our rags there and laid out our food. We sat in a round circle. Alex blessed the food. We served ourselves. It was a delicious meal. Eric stood up and exclaimed, 'You are the big bang, the original force of the universe coming on as Mbiramatako, Mei, Vlarena Leong Alex, our wives and me. When I look at you I see all of you as the same that has existed from before time. The power of the universe rushing on to me. I'm that too. Why spoil it by fearing? By your demise from this earth there is no everlasting non-existence. That's not an experience. We fear being locked up in a narrow dark suffocating coffin, six feet under soil. Or burnt by the sea or river.

Try and imagine what it will be like to go to sleep and never wake up. Now consider this. Eliminate the real sleeping part, concentrate on what you remember as experience only, the going to sleep, we all remember going to sleep, if no dreams, then next thing we remember is waking up. If we dream we experience it, we take part in it and only become aware that it was a dream when we wake up. So the in between of wakefulness and deep sleep, we never experience it though it happens. We only experience the going to and coming from. What is it like to wake up after having never gone to sleep? That is when we are born. It's on and off. It is impossible to experience the physical feel of nothing' 'Mei can you have an experience of nothing?' Alex interrupted Eric. Mei shook her head. Eric continued 'You see, you can't have an experience of nothing. When we die it's just the experience of being us in this present form and life that extinguishes. Life is ever there and will light up again in different form of experience.' Eric was interrupted by a dove that came and perched on the tall Rambutan fruit tree nearby. It started cooing in earnest. 'Amen!' said Eric. We all laughed in unison.

'Remember we said we are all connected in one life form system that switches on and off. So after you're dead or has slept forever, the only thing that can happen is the same experience, or the same sort of experience as when you were born. A new experience awaits every new baby and that experience becomes the person. The person will one day die but life is always there, so another new experience is also ever waiting, which explains the never ending supply of persons or people. Birth is the way life force manifests itself into tangible experience by becoming flesh and blood, which is the person and we will give this new person a name and an environment to grow up in, which will shape and consolidate him into a unique person. The new life force which is the baby cannot talk but can communicate; the life force is very intelligent because it can learn the language in its new environment.' Erich paused talking as he accepted a delicate piece of yellow juicy mango, which his pretty wife dropped into his mouth. He chewed and grunted in satisfaction to the tingling sweet sour taste of the mango.

He resumed, 'It is common knowledge that babies learn language by imitating those around them. Ego is artificial in relation to the real life force that is always present inside the baby. Ego becomes stronger and stronger as the baby grows and follows the norms of its new environment. No wonder adults will ever understand the language of babies because it is sacred language, only spoken by life itself. We call the language baby noises. We are all aware that after other people die other people are born. And they're all us. Only fact is that we can only experience it one at a time. I wonder if there is any living adult who never asked about life and God when they were just young kids. Everybody is I. We all know we're us. And when a baby comes into being that's us coming into being. This is pure love.'

'Imagine if we all become aware of this simple fact and not follow the egoistical instincts of selfishness. There wouldn't be any paedophiles, or wars that kill innocent children and women. Every different society has its own notion of death and fear of death is probably a creation in individual minds.' Alex stood up and said, 'let me come in and add that there are ancient societies who could just bend down and give birth while working in the fields. They would cut the umbilical cord, wrap up the baby, and continue. It wasn't that their women were tougher than ours, but just that they had a different attitude. It used to be thought that childbirth should be painful, as a punishment for Original Sin or for having had so much fun conceiving the baby. For God had said to Eve and all her daughters, in sorrow thou shalt bring forth children. Thus when everyone believed that in having a baby it was a woman's duty to suffer, women did their duty of sufferance, and many still do.'

Alex continued, 'you see most of the things we fear most are creations by society. Our lives could be shortened by death but still it is a grand event. Most people live in life long fear and anxiety about death but the inevitable will happen to all of us. That is the day of reckoning, the day for letting go of the self importance, the ego. In every individual's life, this rare chance comes once. It takes us to the knowledge that one's actual self is the Self which plays the universe, an occasion that calls for much pomp and fanfare, not crying, or maybe crying but crying in joy for our loved one who has become enlightened. That is why we all want an honourable death. So that we go into that realm in honour.'

Our days at the resort were coming to a close. Eric was going back on Monday. Mei looked at me with her lips pouted and complained 'I saw that you have an eager beaver for you to tickle. You never applied oil for me; I always do on my own.' 'Well you never ask me' I replied. Mei was tickled. She became attentive to me. My attraction to Mei was at a peak but I kept it under tight wraps. I didn't want to start drama at this outing. She felt it. We both felt it when we sat together. When the sides of our arms touched briefly, it was electric. Her sharp intake of breath tantalized me. There were times when I felt someone was watching me. I look up. There is Mei staring at me. I try to engage her, she looks aside. I was deep in concentration to Alex or Eric talking. I feel her subtly edge closer to my back. I feel the heat first before I felt her hard erect nipples. Her pubic mound rubs against the naked flesh of my buttocks. I feel intensely uncomfortable. We were nude. If the blood rushed south and kept firing, quite a spectacle would result. I used all my control. Though I break up in a sweat, I manage to control the shaft.

Late afternoon four of us went to bath at the river. Alex and Eric wanted to discuss business. I swam for a long while before creeping to a secluded flat stone with some over hanging bushes giving shade. I lay down to rest. The beauty of this place never ceased to amaze me. The astral rays of asters in white, pale blue roses and coreopsis are rupturing in splendour all around me. Creating a spectrum of beauty everywhere. The cool climate of the surrounding highlands made far off places look misty and mysterious. The incessant chirping of the birds and splash of water were a perfect lullaby. I drifted off. Suddenly I felt a hot moistness on my mouth. I opened my eyes as I became aware of the weight of Mei's shapely butt planted right at my face! How daring! I pretended to struggle. I started to lick lightly, rolling my tongue into a rigid point. Making incessant stabs at the entrance of Mei's vagina. It responded by fluttering continuously. She began to roll and gyrate, her pussy tightly clamped to my mouth. I continued to lick her. I sucked the pink petals gently, until they became swollen and red. She moaned. She practically rode my mouth. Her juices were welling down. I kept pushing out with my tongue to avoid swallowing them. They made a river in between Mei's vaginal lips. I kept at it until I felt her clench and unclench. She released all tension from her body. She lay near me. She touched my member and it literary spurted its stuff. I shook all over. I felt very peaceful. Mei shifted nearer me. She clutched a branch from the bushes and broke it. She covered our bodies with it.

We drifted into a very comfortable sleep. I felt that I would have the proverbial cow slaughtered before we went back. Unfortunately things always get exciting when time is running out. Mei also seemed to feel the excitement in the air. The urgency of the imminent end to our trip. Everyone seemed to feel it. Eric's three wives were very playful. The three of them disappeared into their cabin. It was amazing. Alex and the young beautiful wives were nowhere to be seen. Vlarena and Leong were closer in their relationship. They seemed more subdued and more loving. There was less playful groping. They too had disappeared into their room in the cabin. I felt like me and Mei were the only guests around. I suggested that we also go inside. 'Your cabin or mine?' Mei asked mischievously. We chose my cabin. We hopped in and I immediately clutched Mei's delicate form with hot hands. I ran them along her perfect body contours. It felt electric. My totem pole was very restless. It insisted towards Mei's centre, her moist fire. I was in the right position. Standing together there in the middle of the cabin. I felt her centre yield. I pushed but my progress was stopped by tightness. At the same time Mei screamed in agony. She opened her eyes and disengaged. The spell was broken. She quickly went to the door and went out.

The next day we were all relaxing, stretching out after our morning jog. Later that day we planned to visit an elephant park. We were going to view the butterflies first. At the spot we chose to view the butterflies, Alex pointed and said 'those are Atlas moth and that big butterfly perched there is the Golden birdwing butterfly. There is quite a variety of wild butterfly species around these lands.' They were beautiful creatures. A spectrum of God's love. Eric was looking at butterflies. He said, 'funny how beautiful and innocent life is yet so fragile.' We picked a good spot to set up our picnic and settled. I took several pictures of the big butterflies with my camera. Mei and everyone else took photos too. It was beautiful. We sat down for some food. Eric suggested that he wanted to share with us some interesting psychology experiments done to analyse human behaviour. 'Humans are very tough and at the same time very fragile, so delicately balanced, its no wonder in psychology we discovered that humans are very intelligent but very vulnerable. The Asch Experiment is a popular example of the luring power of the need to fit in within group set ups. The experiments were done in the 1950s. One subject was put in a room of people playing roles of other participants. An image with three lines was put up and everyone was asked which one was the longest. The role players deliberately picked the wrong answer. At first the subject chose correct answers but as the experiment continued he also started choosing wrong answers! Wow you see. Eric paused to take a photo of a big colourful butterfly. 'Do you know that butterflies taste with their feet?'

He continued, 'the other very interesting experiment on human behaviour was unethical but educating. The Stanford Prison experiment set out to find psychological effects of prison setting and how they influence human behaviour. In 1971, a fake prison was constructed in the basement of Stanford University and twenty four male students were chosen to act out as guards and prisoners exchanging for two weeks. The students became real mean and aggressive and even the psychology professor was not spared in his role as superintendent. The experiment was stopped after six days only. Certain situations can bring the unbelievable in us. Be careful hey?' and he laughed.

He proceeded, 'the little Albert experiment also controversial but very valid. The experiment was done in 1921 by John Watson and his partner at Johns Hopkins University. A nine year old boy was made to have unreasonable fears. Watson started by placing a white rat near the boy and he showed no fear. Every time the rat was placed a loud noise was produced to frighten the boy. Later the boy started crying and showing signs of fear whenever the rat appeared in the room. Two more before I call it a day in preaching. Remember its moral violence. So this one is about how unaware people are sometimes, unaware of even their immediate environment. In this experiment a flier was put up by the grocery store with a notice about a missing child and the child in the flier was made to stand nearby. Some people read it some didn't but they all failed to see the child in the flier was nearby wearing the same clothes as in the flier!'

'And the one about people's tendency to blindly obey authority. Stanley Milgram did an experiment in 1963 in which subjects were made teachers and a learner. The teachers were told to give electric shock each time a learner got it wrong and increase shock if the learner continued failing. The subjects continued to give fatal shock as instructed even though they could hear moans of pain from the learner. And they even carried on giving massive shocks even after they were told the leaner had become unconscious! So you see guys we have to be very careful in life. Ok let's go and prepare to go for the trip to the elephant park.' After bath and dressing up we all filed into the cars and went to the elephant park. It was joyful to be so close to those gentle giants. We gave them a bath in a river and fed them. I didn't know the elephant was so huge. I heard loud rumbling from their stomachs. Mei rode one elephant through the jungle after getting instructions on some basic commands on how to handle the elephant.

That evening Alex came and said 'remember I told you that I and my friends are the eccentric three. Well the last one you haven't seen is Joseph. I invited him earlier so that you could meet him but his schedule was full. I guess you are lucky. Joseph is coming for vacation here. He told me on the phone the government in his country is putting intense pressure on him to stop his project. He is involved in a project to rebuilt new cities and transform life into the future. No one in power wants to support him. In the last couple of weeks he went on a crusade to spread his message and vision. He is exhausted and need time to put aside the ego and just be himself. Be here in the natural peace of the resort.'

The next day we went about our routines but we were all expectant. Joseph was coming at 10 am. We sat in Alex's porch. At 10 am he arrived alone. He was old but like his friends a youthful Joseph in an old man's body. He greeted us. He proceeded to take the seat offered to him. We all introduced ourselves. Food and drinks were brought in. Joseph said, 'my idea is that it is now time to wake up and be progressive. We are at a point in time in history when all old ideas are past their use by date. So many ideas that people still cling to are obsolete. People are trying many new religions. I want to warn you not to oppose your adults and parents about religion. It's not worth it to try to prove your smartness by looking down on any religion. Respect diversity and formulate your own path informed by the best knowledge you can find. The biggest difference between the present generation and older generations is that you can do everything as informed by knowledge. Sources of knowledge include your teachers, priests, rabbi and all. Balance it with informed academia and you are a better person within religion and outside of it. Knowledge is liberation. I wish there was a religion that gives me the power to find out answers by experience, as in how we experience to ride a bike or swim. Its exhilarating when we master it and find out it's so easy after all! I come to you with a challenge to find out the best way to balance life between work and pleasure. Remember if you choose the right profession for yourself you never have to work the rest of your life. You'll be productive only.'

'Young people, I want you to appreciate the need to change and move on. The idea of God the creator was invented to control humans but it failed because many today do not believe. Young man, imagine this scenario, you suddenly become aware that all you do is in God's glare He is aware of your most minute feelings and notions. How does it feel? Are you going to be able to carry on and not break his rules? Many now have tried to get rid of God by becoming atheists but they still feel inadequate because when we deny the existence of God it's the same as denying oneself.'

Joseph pointed at me and said, 'young man tell me what did you learn in school that you can use in life? I replied that I learnt mathematics, science and communication. I'm a nurse and am educated in looking after the sick and frail. 'Sounds impressive but I want to tell you about the future, great concepts for the future, I envision a future with humans living free of disease and living long lives, maybe even past hundred and thirty. I think that now is the time for action to change the world. We have enough theories around. Let's try something that can be applied immediately. The future is now, and young people I'm sure you are all aware of the Wall Street crash and how people lost billions of money. Today you are well off, tomorrow you are utterly penniless and your house repossessed. What kind of nightmares are we living? We cannot cling to this way simply because it benefits certain elites. We have to bid so long a lasta vista to the monetary system. We need a real wealth based system of economy. We need to use the resources that we have and not money.'

We planned to visit the night market in the city but we decided to go in daylight. We wanted to have a quality last night together. The next morning the whole group shared cars and we drove into the city. I'd not experienced so much beauty and variety before. The city was a spectrum of colours, red, bright orange and pink and purple. There was a variety of flowers on sale including the voluptuous tropical flowers, like jasmine, orchids and lotus buds. Alex explained the legend of the famous temple on top of the mountain 'Wat Phra That Doi Suthep was constructed in 1383 during the Lanna Thai period, it is believed that the temples site was picked by an elephant sent to roam the mountain, whose name is Doi Suthep, where upon reaching a suitable spot, it trumpeted, circled three times, knelt down and promptly died. This was interpreted as a sign indicating an auspicious site.' Alex showed us the Ping River whose tributary ran through his property. The Bhuping Royal Palace Gardens were 4 km further along the road from Wat Prathat. There were many shops selling local handicrafts. We paid 10 baht to enter a flower garden. Mei and all the other women in our party took turns to take pictures wearing traditional clothes. We walked into Chang Klan Rd, the famous Night Bazaar. We saw a lot of hotels and guest houses. In Loi Kroh Rd which is the centre of the city's night life was presently quiet. We all took a break to eat bowls of kao soi. Later Mei bought an umbrella from Bo Sang. Other streets Alex showed us and said, 'Ratchadamneon Rd is popular for Sunday night exploration of the market from Tha Phae Gate to the popular Wat Phra Singh. The temple delights in grand scenery over the city.' Our group took the cable car for 20 baht each to experience for ourselves what Alex had described to us. We all agreed that it was awesome. We went back to the resort feeling high in spirits!

That night Alex lit the fire in his porch. It was very welcome. There was a keen wind. It was overcast and dark. We were all dressed in warm but light clothing. We relaxed in Alex's porch. It was me

Leong, Vlarena, Mei, Alex and his two wives, Eric and his three wives and Joseph. The golden liquor was out. Bowels of steaming meats and eats were set. I noticed some green grapes with dew on them. My mouth watered. We attacked the goodies with great gusto. Joseph threw a small thigh of baby chicken into his mouth whole. He licked his finger, turned to me and gestured 'Mbiramatako I hope you show us the magic of your talisman.' I nodded yes. Every one was curious to hear me play the mbira. It was a mystery to them. I took my mbira from Mei and told her laughing, 'in my culture women are not supposed to handle important equipment like this.' She discreetly gave me the finger and laughed. I settled into position. I did my thing. I began with simple projections, dungy, mambo, muzzy, going on. Mei knew precisely when to join in with her flute. We had the advantage of endless rehearsal when we played back in China in that apartment. The harmony of the mbira delicately mixed with wafts of the flute bloomed into endless tunes. We engaged to my most favoured tune by Kris Kristofferson and Chiwoniso Maraire called 'The Circle, Song For Layla A Attar and Los Olivadios.' I felt numb to every thing else except the heat of my thumb and index finger as they rubbed the steel blades of the mbira. The level of rhythm that we reached calls down spirits to celebration with humans. I felt the spirit of Chaminuka envelope me. It urged me on in courage and full glory in the far away mountains of Chiang Mai. The power was unmistakeable. For that moment there was total harmony between the spirit realm and humans. Suddenly we were all startled by the flash of lightning and the clap and rumble of thunder. As if to drown that out Mei started clapping. Everyone joined in. She continued her flute. It became the melody of the mbira, flute and the rain! The rain poured. We never stopped until I felt my hands no more. The two member acoustic band was unleashed. It was an intense rhythm. It reached a crescendo. We slowly broke it down. There was total quiet. Only the incessant croak of the bullfrogs at the river and the raindrops making dripping sounds as they fell from the huge tees around us. The air was fresh with the remnant of the smell of burnt rice, acrid dying vegetation and the sweet scent of various flowers like the petunia, lilies and the famous orchids. It was an exotic smell. Alex was quiet for a while. Looking down. He raised his head, 'that was powerful. It usually doesn't rain in May.'

Next morning Alex sat with us inside the house. He said in sober tones, 'you came here for vacation. It turned out to be the biggest learning experience of your lives. We are reborn of mind and spirit, enlightened. What do we do? We go on living a purposeful, fulfilling life backed by certain knowledge of ourselves. We shall confront the trappings of this world with wisdom. We know it's a concrete jungle, this life on earth. We will dance on. Contribute in our own little ways. Add more spirit than cement. Remember there is a power that is all of us, a loving, caring power. May you shine in positive rays. I must say your acoustic act will remain etched in my old brilliant brain. There is an event that happened to Dr Eben Alexander when he had brain infection and went into coma for a week. He experienced the extraordinary. It's up to you all and me to analyse what he has to say. Think deeply. Reflect on what other great philosophers in time say about this. His story goes'

'God has no gender; in fact I did not use God in my writing because the power and the awe of that Deity, all loving, all powerful Deity is beyond any words at all.' In response to weather he really saw God he said, 'I became everything that God was showing me and that's when I first glimpsed the divine that was all through everything and the loving presence. It was knowing that the divine and infinitely powerful Creator of all was everywhere and I just, it was my noticing it that divine was all of that. That presence was in everything, everything in my awareness and right after that the entire scene, it just collapse and there was this brilliant orb of light and the orb of light was brighter than a million suns right there in my awareness.' How could he look at it? 'Easily, easily because it was all the energy of everything throughout all time. I was not limited by any physical attributes at all infact by this point this was not Eben Alexander's consciousness, this was all consciousness throughout all eternity throughout higher multiversity being one with that divine all powerful, all loving Creator. God does not have a face nor gender and is awesome beyond any words I could possibly use to describe. And when I was in this higher dimensional, what I call the core, which was the infinite blackness but with this brilliant orb of light and with that divine loving presence every where, there was the sound of Om but it had no beginning and end. It was the resonance of that sound given the fact that I was in the infinite space, infinite dimension and all of eternity and that resonance sounded like Om and that's why I call that divine entity Om, God is way too small, it's so limiting.'

Mei unlocked the front door to the apartment. We all flocked inside. We missed the shimmering bells, the alluring purple walls, the charming chandeliers. The sensuous smell of the wild flower. The cool breeze swinging the white lace curtains. It felt good to be home. We refreshed and rested in a rather pensive mood. Leong and Vlarena were not playful as they usually were. I went down to the mart. I bought some drinks and a few supplies for the house. The Chinese shop assistant smiled. He said 'today no Carlsberg boss?' 'No another day' I replied. On my return I met Pathma. He seemed more bended. It took a while before he responded to my greeting. I kept eye contact. He said 'ah, ayah, that's you. My eyesight is failing me. How're you? You look trim and healthy and content. I didn't see you in a long while. I bet you went for a holiday with that Dame. You slaughtered your cow right?' he gave a full toothless smile. 'No Pathma no luck but I had a splendid holiday.' 'Never mind. Do not desire. In good time the cow will come to you. You will slaughter your cow. It shall be worth the wait. I'm sure.' Pathma said. He patted me on the back. I said bye and went up.

As I entered the apartment I was surprised to hear music wafting out seductively. Usually we played different music than this. I went inside. Mei was sitting in the sofa her legs folded underneath her. She liked this posture. 'What song is that playing?' I asked her as I passed her a tin of low fat yoghurt. 'It's by Barbara Streisand and Ray Charles, 'Crying Time.' How did you know I was craving yoghurt?' she peeled the foil off and licked it ever so slightly. I liked to watch her do that, which is why I had bought the yoghurt for her. 'Instincts!' I smiled at her and proceeded to the kitchen. We prepared dinner and took it in silent comfort. We all sat and relaxed. 'So what do you all think of the trip to Chiang Mai?' Mei asked. 'It was beyond words, it was splendid, thanks for arranging that. My mind is still a buzz plus I feel a certain way. I cannot really describe it. Call it wise presence. I don't know' I said. I felt curiously aware of something. I could not pin down and name it. I felt that life was too much of an experience to ever limit oneself on one rigid idea. That is very limiting. Declarations were made daily from the science community and the spiritual side. They thought that they got it at last. It all fizzled out. Life goes on. The knowledge that I got from Chiang Mai was sacred. It gave me a new life. I became a new person without anyone prodding me to. Everything naturally followed a pattern towards more questions and answers and wisdom. I learnt that you haven't started anything in this world unless you discover the human. There is nothing new under the sun except the individual experience of humans.

The journey of discovery goes on. Let's learn from the journey. The answer lies with the individual. The more we are able to decode the mystery that is the human, the better placed we are to find out about life A world free of war and suffering is possible if the world concentrate more on knowing the self than defending one's beliefs. The energy we spend convincing ourselves and others and even fighting for beliefs, should go to peaceful meditation. It is very tempting to say lets get rid of religion that binds men to dogma and useless doctrines but it's not as easy as that. I was holding a Chinese daily press and parts of the article went,

Wang Zuoan, head of the State Administration of Religious Affairs, said there had been an explosion of religious belief in China along with the nation's economic boom, which he attributed to a desire for reassurance in an increasingly complex world.

While religion could be a force for good in officially atheist China, it was important to ensure people were not mislead, he told the Study Times, a newspaper published by the Central Party School which trains rising officials.

"For a ruling party which follows Marxism, we need to help people establish a correct world view and to scientifically deal with birth, ageing, sickness and death, as well as fortune and misfortune, via popularizing scientific knowledge," he said, in rare public comments on the government's religious policy.

"But we must realize that this is a long process and we need to be patient and work hard to achieve it," Wang added in the latest issue of the Study Times, which reached subscribers on Sunday. "Religion basically upholds peace, reconciliation and harmony . . . and can play its role in society," Wang said.

"But due to various complex factors, religion can become a lure for unrest and antagonism. Looking at the state of religion in the world today, we must be very clear on this point."

CHAPTER 9

Earlier, when I was younger mom told me that my good fortune lay in me going up a mountain. 'Why mom? I don't want to climb a mountain.' She told me she dreamt it. And to mom it meant making a journey to a real mountain in any of the favoured sports by the faith sects. I think her dream told her that I had to go far away from home to attain my fortune. But it was given in her familiar context as a mountain. I got my wisdom in the mountains of Chiang Mai. In a sense her dreams were correct. Only maybe a little misinterpreted by her. A lot of thoughts were churning in my head. I'm reminded of Edward Leedskalnin's coral castle. He built it from 1923 to 1951. He declared that he had decoded the secret of the builders of the Egyptian pyramids. He had a small book in which he wrote about magnetism. He used to leave blank pages so that if there was any one who did not agree with him, they could put down their own theories in the blank pages. Blank page couldn't be more further from his brain. He was a small man and this happened in modern times in the US. He began building but changed the place. He loaded the lorry by himself. Huge boulders of stone. The driver of the lorry was told to go and come back at a certain time. He came earlier and was surprised to see the lorry half full already!

At the new place he built the coral castle. It still stands today in magnificent awe. This awesome guy discovered the ancients' secret. He managed to do the extraordinary. One day my mom told me to use lemon water to reduce my body acidity levels. She told me this knowledge was passed down to her. I did not listen to her. I knew lemon was sour and acidic to litmus testing. Years later I discovered that yes indeed lemons in water alkalize our bodies. When it is absorbed by the body it alkalises the body. Thereby keeping it healthy. The real secret to any belief or religion is to find out why they practice certain rituals. The answers give a lot of insight about the beliefs.

I dreaded a phantom spirit coming into me. Being possessed like what I see in voodoo practices. I prefer a practice that clarifies me as an individual. Help me to understand myself, before I attempt to understand others. How about my Christian teachings and what Alex said. Jesus taught, 'I am the light of the world, the I am, the only way to God. Alex said, 'We can look at Life as interplay of pulses or tremors with a particular arrangement of neurons also known as nerve cells. The pulses or vibrations produced by the sun become light and heat when they interplay and interact with a living organism. Jesus said, 'I am the resurrection and the life, Before Abraham was I am. If you have seen me, you have seen the Father.' Eric said 'You see, you can't have an experience of nothing. So when we die it's just the experience of being us in this present form and life that extinguishes. Life is ever there and will light up again in different form of experience. Remember we said we are all connected in one life form system that switches on and off. After you're dead or has slept forever, the only thing that can happen is the same experience, or the same sort of experience as when you were born. Jesus represents love. He preferred to reach out to the less savoured society such as prostitutes and lepers. He never craved power or self aggrandisement. Jesus' mentored, 'Come, follow and obey me.' He absolved sin. He was the most misunderstood and still is.

It is written that he referred to himself as 'Before Abraham was, I am if you have seen me, you have seen the Father.' He said 'I am "God incarnate" and the life; he who believes in me, though he is dead, yet shall he live.' He is also attributed with saying, 'I am the light of the world, the I am, the only way to God, I am the "truth." Philip asked Jesus to show them the Father. Jesus said, "Philip, have I been with you so long and you don't know me?' Inevitably he was accused of blasphemy. Jesus pointed out, 'The Son of Man has authority on earth to forgive sins.' Leaders in Jesus' time told him they were going to kill him because, 'you, a mere man, have made yourself God.' Jesus' alluding himself to God's name greatly angered the religious leaders. He was claiming to be God, the Creator of the universe! They missed a crucial point about Jesus. I'm sure even today we are still stumbling in the dark. Trying to decipher the mystery of Jesus. In simplicity complexity shrouds. Limitations to the human faculty abound.

Leong interrupted my stream of thoughts. 'Hey, hey guys actually I saw a book with information about a story that Time and space seem to be endless because they are both converted within a constantly changing system. All intelligence in the cosmos meets from different directions at an odd trait of singularity through black holes at both big and small magnitudes. Time is the frequency at which the intelligence exchanges between the singularity and the watcher in connection to the watcher's distance from it. Black holes are an opening to a magnificent origin of energy and awareness which we understand as God. It is an opening amidst heaven and earth, a window across all there exists and all that will exist. Existence therefore, all we are and all things we see is founded on the meeting up or convergence of two electro magnetic forces which when united, produce a third of equilibrium and a principal source of creational energy (singularity).'

I still hoped to get the perfect love from Mei. I perceived she was perfect in character. Two individuals two independent ways of thinking trying to find common ground. Love hurt due to the issue of adjusting to each other. I've many friends who divorced because of differences in religious belief, temperament differences and even incompatible sexual drives and sexual orientation. To get along there has to be an agreement. If both want to be superior and get their own way then all drama unfolds. The perfect love has got someone submitting. With me and Mei we both wanted the other to be totally equal. We hoped for harmony with each other.

It seemed an impossibility to be on equal terms in love and still be in love. When you reach the level of being perfectly equal in love, it's no longer a love relationship as we know it. More of a special trusting phenomenon. Mei preferred us not to declare that we loved each other. She said that would bring complications in the form of loyalty. She abhorred the entanglements of a committed partnership. No freedom and lots of jealousy. Sharing moments just as colleagues can be very rewarding and satisfying. This explains why sometimes husbands have mistresses and wives lovers because there is sweet sharing without the loyalty and burden of staying together until death do them part. Both Alex and Eric didn't seem to give their wives any rules. They did everything according to their discretion. They partook in all the indulgencies we did. Those who did not enjoy certain activities were free to declare so. Alex's other wife did not drink nor smoke. She enjoyed everything else though.

What Alex and the other eccentric two had taught us was that humans are one with God. The whole universe instead of seeking favours from God could practice those favours all around us. Loving and caring for ourselves and others and the universe. Same as we would expect God to do to all creation. We could celebrate creation in oneness with God. That would mean no discrimination on race, religion and gender. No hatred, no dogmas that imprison us. No rituals detached from reality. Dogmas that preach if you are not like us you don't belong and must be cut off from one another can be gently laid down to rest. We can agree that we are all from different regions of the earth. We have different beliefs. Let's meet and learn from each other. The world is interesting in its natural spectrum of differences that come from the same and goes back to the same. The world does not need a conquering religion or superpower. Instead of amassing weapons and logistics for fatal troop movements in the world, let's organise exchange programmes throughout the world. Whereby school kids exchange and learn other societies and appreciate the other. Let's have a world that is decorated by people prepared to be in each other's shoes. That way the word will walk in peace.

The concept of being proud of our nationality is quite great. Proud to be American! Proud to be Chinese! Or proud to be African! I read a story on our way back to China. It was about one us soldier in Afghanistan who was stabbed in the neck by a militant boy whilst he was playing with local children. The assailant escaped. The US soldier lost life. We cannot rely on patriotism to co survive. Unnecessary life is lost because of differences in ideology. We cannot do without life. We can do without ideology. How wonderful it would be one day to hear, 'proud to be human!' I propose that we need new ideas! What is needed is to recognise that people in power are fewer than the majority in plain numbers. Currently the smaller number makes decisions for the bigger number. It should work like this, the bigger number must make decisions and the smaller number comply and implement. There is power in the individual. One small strike burnt forests later. The common man has never sat down and pushes all pressures, all problems aside and tries to find out how powerful he can be. Again that calls for innovation. There is no hope in the politicians unless you are connected to the system. The common man can triumph against even weapons of mass destruction because he can infiltrate and work closer to the enemy. A nuclear bomb or hydrogen bomb cannot be used in one's own turf otherwise it will kill the master also.

Instead of contemplating war and confrontation, why not try the way of love. Where we don't need big guns as big Ids. Soldiers, policemen and everyone is someone's son or daughter brother or sister. We all represent the other. The one that you shoot and torture is representative of you. Why fight against thyself?! It's only that we think we are immune to the pain the other feels. Consider the last scene from the movie, 'The Last Samurai' starring Tom Cruise. The superior army slug the other which was out numbered and poorly equipped but very courageous. The army slugged and slugged them with bullets. They kept coming and dying. In the end the superior army took off their hats in pained salute and honour to the fallen Katsumoto who had committed seppuku. The agony of Katsumoto was written all over their faces! The other only looks and appears different so that we can be sure of our own self. Not so that we fight him. When I was a kid at Grandma Chihwiza's farm, I used to explore and forage the thick bushes around. It was quite often that I met strange looking creatures. Especially in the rainy season. I saw a strange looking worm with hairs all over and a fiery temper. If I handled it my hand would blister and be itchy. Each time I met such a strange insect my instinct was to attack it. Many innocent creatures faced demise by my hand. I took their strangeness for a threat. Imagine a world living in homogenous state. Looking and thinking alike. No variety whatsoever. Everywhere you look you see only shimmering white forms. What a grey world it will become.

My stomach churns in pain and my heart bleeds in the wish that one day there could be peace in the world. It all begins with the individual heart. My country is faced with an imminent election. It's natural for the turtle to breath through their rear ends and they live very long. It is equally true that the human brain is only 2% of a person's body mass but requires 20% of oxygen and calories from the body. This shows how powerful the human brain is. Humans should not think through their rear. It's not natural to them. They must utilize the terrific brain to architect the country. I beg to appeal to all to practice restraint and exude love at this great possibility to shape the country. The desire is to have peace and prosperity, not death and destruction.

Desideratum

The body politic is porous
Elucidation is to aggregate on one Dark horse
Ace conveyance is as inconscient as the national
    currency

Impetus for innovation accosted by lack of suitable
    nominee
Is balked but despair not, muse ad hoc
Proviso atrophy, brackish
Adjudge if seductive to endure
That is tremendous beacon, the rest
Is rationale

Body politic is alert to duress in the pub
On the boulevard, in the village, sans provocation
Royalty is fetid in dirt and claret
Decrepit the extreme dregs of dash,
Wallop of a moribund burro begrudgingly to score
By a band of contentious laggards
The adversary, puerile partially proven
Enamoured and rash, capricious in prattle
He could be the diamond with a flaw rather
Than that perfect pebble

Inordinate devotion is intercept of the canon of qualm
Avail arcane cull to lull affliction
Laconic cardinals cognate ants to crumb an elephant
Adulation will manifest in conquest over
    consternation!
How alluring the revival of refinement
In the neoteric comb not crown or eloquence of accent
Gross politicians are outlaws in office
A Robin Hood in tie and jacket will suffice
Nectarous is the affiance of conversion, nevermore awry
The modish affirm to be old in contrivance
Politician is best beheld akin to the Egyptian cobra
Keep looking him right in the eye

I want to acknowledge the current President of my country. It is very tempting to criticise but he has always faced a surmountable task. Right from soon after independence when sceptics abound. It was like an experiment with many dooms day predictors. He conquered. The West pestered his government to embark on economic reforms. He resisted. They put pressure until government relented. About his dictatorial tendency I understand him. Many times when I am in discussion about Africa it is often that the most passionate guys, the ones with strong aspirations for Africa, will declare that they wish they had the power to just go it alone and achieve their vision. It's not as easy as that. A Look at the current situation concerning the impending election for example. There is acrimony with endless disagreements. The President declared an affirmative decision. Opposition A cry foul saying other opposition is agreeing too prematurely. The other opposition, B gives an obscure comment about it from a conference down in South Africa. It's a mess. That is why certain men, a pragmatic man will just go ahead and lead for thirty three years! There really isn't anyone who could do it better.

Eminence

Preeminence shouldn't consign in situ that cathedra
Deprecate to colossal stature
President way too bantam
Bigger Bird lean not on the grain stalk, it careen
Eminence harmonize caliph, body politic artisan
Life counsel, virtual avant garde
Eminence executed adamantine
Borne gore of brat to brush
Exclusive to you unrivalled,
To endure perpetually in power
You bulldoze body politic habitat, none fret
You accord acreage to natives, stupendous feat

Ever done by any Baron
Sundry discern not the congenial act for the agrarian
Arduous to decree aggregation of rank 'n' file,
Some erudite, aught of acumen others apt to assail
Bygone crackerjack pants closely to nape
Aggravating to reign the game
Aversion kindred a vulture was born, to evince blemish
You beat all odds, ordained to rule
Consistently devoted to efficacy
Like a dove you croon the one clique anthem

Anon autonomy you fostered
Comp, coaching, billet, craft, dignity in personage
The flower of civility, not Cecil Rhodes
Your keen, tenacity is agitative
I scaled the Musasa tree to cut a peek
When you crashed my constituency
Gallant in radiant armour, ubiquity of a lion

Forthwith intellect decrepit, it gallivant
Superfluous in addled dynasty
Archetypal turtle goes speculum
Mirror, mirror on the wall, who is thy smoothest of
    all turtles!
Abettor posit world with anosognosic vista
To do the astute, abdicate the utmost beloved
To consign it love

The ideas that Alex and Joe talked about at the naturist resort
kept staring me in the eye. They remain attractive and refreshing.
They are unlike contemporary ones. The problem comes when we
ask for proof to verify what they propose. The proof would probably
lie in meditation. They concluded that awareness is the only way.
It's very good. It empowers the individual to experience it. A big

difference from praying with eyes closed, kneeling down, addressing no one. However more needs to be done in terms of scientific research by independent scientists. Let's have authoritative literature and textbooks. They can be utilised in school as social sciences.

The idea of the human being one with God will soon become dogma unless it is clarified. People need to eliminate fear and start to live a new way of life. The way of indiscriminate love. If everyone's wish was granted and the guy that I really hated and wanted dead could die if I so wished, I would ask for him to die very fast. There is a big chance someone out there cannot stand my sight, if their wish is granted they'd have me dead in an instant. Unchecked hate will consume us until there is nothing. Is it possible to have 'practical religion'? Instead of grouping to see one man perform miracles for everyone, you go on your own and discover the miracle yourself. The taste of tobacco is in smoking it. You can never describe it to someone adequately.

I realise how Mei worked it out. She didn't want to preach to me. She desired me to experience a journey that has unexpected happenings. I evaluate my thoughts. I confront my self on important issues in life. The topic of interracial relationship comes up. I always maintain that I hate labels. We are two people in love. Some people see an interracial couple instead. When I go out with Mei, it's very uncomfortable. All eyes on us. A relationship will involve others as it becomes stronger. Relatives can ask questions about mixed relationship. My trip to Chiang Mai had made it clear that humans are one and the same entity. Differences in colour only help us to identify ourselves from others. I can easily explain my position with Mei and be understood. I was comfortable with an interracial relationship. I didn't want to court exactly as my grandfather had done. Mei certainly didn't want to go through the same courtship process her grandmother had gone through in the early nineteenth century. To know and enjoy the other completely represented interracial union.

Me and Mei represented pure love that transcends colour or any labels and prejudices. I recognise how similar in character Mei is to Godmother. They both think of 'small' things that most people overlook. Mei thought ahead and made sure I become aware of myself. Of others that surround me before we embark together in love. She did not want me to lust after her beauty. Beauty fades. The human spirit endures beyond death. Love with awareness of human nature is keen and real. It celebrates the beauty of love first. Physical beauty is secondary. Probably Mei wants to avoid the way of Seal and Heidi Klum who divorced after they represented hope to people like me. They reflected what looked like a happy union.

I find it easier to make decisions. I am hopeful that I will be cool in my relationships with others. I'm not cool with having Mei as a friend. I love her too much to start liking her. I'm not sure what tomorrow will bring me. I hope for Mei in the cool winds of May. I'm not sure where I stand with her. I tried my best to let go of any hope on Mei. I decided to let Mei do the nude painting of me.

The next day Mei decreed that the painting start immediately. The venue was her room. It was convenient for her. All equipment was in the room. She was in a jovial mood. She skipped about in her tight pants. We got on by Mei taking time to instruct me on my pose, postures and demeanour. She mixed her paints and talked about laying down sports of colour. I sat as instructed and kept quiet. Mei soon got absorbed. I became quiet. A very long interval passed before Mei covered her work. She told me to take a break. We went to the kitchen and rummaged in the refrigerator for something to bite. Mei made some cold turkey breast sandwiches. We took that with glasses of milk. We felt nourished and refreshed. The house felt very peaceful.

'You know Mei, I remember watching on TV one famous scientist, Richard Dawkins. He was confronting a popular reverend on what he told the people to make them come in large numbers to his congregation. The reverend was jovial. He warned Dawkins not to be aggressive in his message. He was famous and close to President George Bush. He was composed. I was surprised to see in another clip, the same reverend looking pensive and sombre doing an interview about his fall from grace. The issue was that he was accused of homosexual improprieties. Which reminds me are you truly going to be lesbian for the rest of your life? I view lesbians and homosexuals and all in between, the transsexuals, male prostitutes, female prostitutes, as just people doing something different from what I do. I think the problem comes with labels. Once we label people we tend to be prejudiced against them.' Mei looked at me. She replied 'I agree with you. I'm not bound by labels and expectations. I follow what I want at that time when I want to.'

We spent one month of a meditative journey through the painting of the Mbiramatako. It was a private closed door encounter. Me in naked pose and Mei with a brush in her hands. At times she was deliberately provocative. Some days she dressed in a smart business suit, grey. She was serious that day. At times she became motherly. She fed me pancakes the whole day.

On one Tuesday morning the sun was bright. There was a breeze that moved the lace curtains and made the bells chime softly. Mei was ready for the painting to start. I went inside her room and took position at the settee. She was wearing a green silk morning gown. It was flimsy. I liked the way it outlined her figure. Her mood was sultry and sensuous. The past two days she was very sexual but her mood blue. I suspected her hormones were firing high. Her posture was provocative without her putting effort. Many moods of Mei.

The painting progressed. She changed personalities during the course of the painting. The result was indeed a masterpiece that reflected all her moods. Remarkable how her mood swings were captured in her painting of me. 'Let's make this painting a little witchy like Charles Manson instructed to his followers when they committed murder. People are always craving for the witchy isn't it?' Mei said softly as she put final touches to the painting. The complete painting was great. She adorned it with a skull at the corner. 'What the hell is a skull doing on my painting?' I wanted to know. Mei replied, 'this, Mbiramatako is your memento mori, your life story. This is you minus the ego. The spirit of Mbiramatako!'

The next morning I rose early. I couldn't sleep. Mei kept repeating one song over and over again. 'I hate you then I love you' by Celine Dion and Luciano Pavarotti. The song disturbed me. 'Please for Christ's sake enough of Luciano Pavarotti!' I complained to Mei. I went out to the balcony for fresh air. I stood there taking in the fresh air until I felt light headed. I went back inside. Mei was standing there in her white flimsy gown. Her soft thighs were visibly concealed by the gown. I saw the dark triangle beneath the flimsy material. She was not wearing panties. Her lips looked red and slightly swollen. She didn't have lipstick. Her hair shimmered in the rays of the fresh morning sun. She looked fresh as the morning. 'Are you alright? I see you and I see a restless man. Why Mbiramatako?' I told her, 'Of late I'm having vivid dreams of my grandma's lost inheritance. In the dreams she's telling me that she left a secret buried near the granite stone tower. She told me its treasure but did not elaborate weather its money or what. She left a farm for us. We allowed it to be taken by strangers. I feel that I need to go back and right a wrong. Else I will remain a man without inheritance. My grandma, Chihwiza told me before she died, 'you have a family home already.' Mei was quiet for a while. She said, 'if a man decides his destiny, no one should stop him. For it will be a unique journey, a self fulfilling dream. The ball is in your court Mbiramatako.' I did not have money to start any big project. By taking back my inheritance I would be rich instantly.

One day Mei went out in her car. She came back later with a package. She had received it at the national courier. It was from Alex. She went into her room and locked the door. She came out, looked at me and burst into tears. I was confused. I went and held her. I noticed she was laughing. She said 'I'm so happy. I can rest at peace knowing you have something in your life! Look what Alex has sent to you.' She gave it to me. It was a necklace pendant of the orchid flower finished off in 24 carat gold. I was speechless. I was not an expert on jewellery. The feel of it was unlike anything I have ever held in my hand. Mei later explained to me that it was a very rare piece of original ancient jewellery. Carved with wisdom by the ancients. It was price less. If I was ever to sell it she estimated it at millions of dollars. I was armed with my zebra mask, my talisman the mbira, a very rare pendant from ancient times and my painting by Mei. My memento mori. I felt wealthy. I was broke with no savings in the bank. Mei still kept the painting, the 'Mbiramatako' in her room. She suggested that she would keep it at her friend's gallery. The right conditions for its preservation existed there. The painting shocked us in its brilliant beauty. We started the idea in play. We never thought such a seriously exquisite piece of art would come out of it.

A feud was brewing between me and Mei. She claimed it was her piece of work. I was the model. Besides she had given it to me upon its completion. Mei was crazy. She stuck to the painting. I doubted if I was ever going to see and touch it again. The issue of money made Mei come up with a brilliant idea which she, only saw advantage in. She suggested that we sell the 'Mbiramatako' and split the proceeds. That way I could get away with hundreds of thousands if not millions. I laughed and said 'please Mei, I know we all agreed the 'Mbiramatako' is a spectacular piece of art. To say it can fetch up to a million bucks? Don't you think that's a bit too far fetched? Besides I want my painting. I want to keep my memento mori.'

Mei looked at me defiantly. She asserted, 'my friend at the gallery informed me the 'Mbiramatako' is getting quite good enquiries. I'm quite sure that painting is priceless given time.' I interjected, 'my point exactly! Given time, I will keep it till the end of time!' I shouted at Mei. She lost her temper but controlled herself. I could see the small clenched fist. I moved to a safe distance and said, 'call Leong and Vlarena and ask their opinion.' They came and after a while they both said Mei should give me the painting as per promise. She shouted at us and stormed out into her room. She banged the door in our faces. We were left dumbfounded. In the end she did not sell it. She informed me that one private collector had taken it to display in his gallery. For a certain period and return it to Mei. Then back to me. I doubted very much her story. It kept me quiet. Mei suggested for me to stay in the country with them. Try to work out something good.

'There is good advantage for you here than in your country.' Mei tried to cajole me. 'Don't look down my country' I barked at her and she glared back at me. She was not impressed.

It was Thursday afternoon. Mei was excited. She showed me the photos the art collector had sent her. It was the 'Mbiramatako', displayed in his gallery in Dubai! 'God I'm in Dubai!' I went and swept the delicate form of Mei into my arms. I lifted her off her feet and planted a light kiss on her pouted expectant cherry pink lips! I realised the powerful magic of Mei. She had connections all over the world. If she was not known by the owner of the art gallery in Dubai, the 'Mbiramatako' would never have been there. I knew Mei had quite a lot of money. She could probably sponsor me in anything I wanted to do. For a strange reason she never offered. I never asked!

The next day I bid farewell to Leong and Vlarena. It was quite emotional. I felt a painful gob in my throat. I desperately wanted to cry. It just happens. Having stayed together for quite some time it was hard to say goodbye. Vlarena held me tightly in her arms. Tears streamed down her sweet cheeks. She said, 'I know one day we will meet again, I'm quite sure!' I told her 'I wrote a poem for you, I deliberately changed roles to ease my pain of leaving, it goes',

Sweet Vlarena

No more will the sun incandesce,
If sweet Vlarena were to leave
Notions of sorrow and vexatious cogitation
Affliction twists and turns the heart, relentless smarting
Oh, sorrow the sweet savour of cantaloupe
Oh, sweet reminisce of Vlarena, pain at migration
Hunches sorrowful and aberrant, corrupt
To the fragile core, vulnerable and bereft
Of sweet Vlarena

CHAPTER 10

In the history of mankind there are some individuals who stood out and made great changes to history, whether negative or positive. Men who had a calling and stood out for what they believed in and archived it. Men like, Nelson Mandela, R G Mugabe, J Nkomo, Ayatollah Khomeini, and Mahathir of Malaysia. Mahathir Ghandi, Lenin, Mao tse Tung, Barack Obama, Bob Marley, Abraham Lincoln, These men responded to the unique calling that makes us resolute and carries on despite tremendous odds opposing us. I felt it in every inch of my muscular body. I needed to build my own coral reef like EDL. Against all odds, I would lift huge boulders of responsibility. Sacrifice and triumph. Trump aside, nothing was going to stop me. I was lean and kicking, clean and squeaking.

When the arrow's need for meat becomes too great to bear, it will spring from the bow on its own. It was automatic for me that I had to go and right a wrong done. The obsession I once had for Mei was great. Equal to that was my need to go back and reclaim my lost inheritance. I went home without the 'Mbiramatako.' I figured out that once I recovered our farm I could somehow make it work. When I reached home reality hit me straight in the face. Instead of a hero's welcome I got a horror welcome on my family's faces. They were happy I was back home. Deep down everyone knew the reality of settling down. Of finding a job in a country with a struggling economy. I was optimistic. I set about looking for nurse vacancies.

Meanwhile I told mom I intended to reclaim our heritage. She told me that grandma Chihwiza's farm was a no go area. It had been taken over by the liberation war veterans of the seventies. I asked my friend to help me by driving me to Chihwiza farm. I took along my cousin.

I wanted to talk and negotiate with the rag tags occupying the farm. We reached by gravel. We saw small bands of men in yellow overalls milling around the farm. Some were setting irrigation pipes. The activity was limited to another area of the farm. 'Good.' I thought to myself. The area where I was interested in was still intact. The trees and vegetation had been ravaged. The basic landmarks were still there. It was not disturbed much. It was rocky and could not sustain cultivation. There was another reason which I later heard from the leader. I went straight to him because he looked different. He was dressed in brown trousers and grey shirt not overalls. I told him I had an important issue so we went and sat under the Muchakata tree. I told him my story. He replied that the place with the conical stone was believed to be haunted. I proposed to the man that we share the farm and I take the piece with the tower. He was immediately incensed and raised his voice. 'Is this why you come here? To invade this land? Let me tell you. Today you have roasted your beef on smoke. It's charred!' as he shouted this he lunged at my friend. He punched him straight on the mouth. He targeted him because he was tall and fat and represented the most threat. He is not strong. He doesn't exercise and this guy is a farmer, fit. My friend flew and sat hard on his butt, stunned. My cousin frantically ran to the car, fumbled and couldn't find the keys. The rest of the mob had surrounded us. They were whistling and closing in on us. Wisps of a dusty trail pervaded. I was confused whether they wanted to attack or to stop their boss from hitting us. My friend stood still in daze. I could see his eye was on the car. He attempted to run towards it. The mob was upon him. They tripped him in a style called 'skuna' in the locale. He went down face first. I felt my stomach turn. In the end I got off scot free. The mob took us to the local police. We were charged for disorderliness. I had tried. It had cost my friend an unnecessary beating. In the aftermath of this incident I chilled and settled into normal routine. Going to work come back. Go to the local pub with my childhood friends and come back home. If mom was still awake I sit and chat with her. She has a lot of fears. She fears an in law from hell. I tell her that I will spare her the pain of a new in law. I told her that I was not going to get married. I was in love with a mermaid and she was far away in dreamland. A year had passed already. I did not even realise it. I'm only aware of the constant veil of gloom of memory of Mei. It was going to be hard to erase her. I also missed the 'Mbiramatako.'

I knew getting back grandma Chihwiza's farm was a formidable task I conceded that I had hit a brick wall. Failure is failure, you cannot undo pregnancy by coughing. I was in the doldrums. I was dejected. I felt like my whole life was useless. I felt like I wanted to go into my small room and sleep in my bed for a long time. I didn't want to do anything at all. I was very high up in hope and the fall knocked the breath out of me. It was a bitter symphony without any sweetness.

I am dissipated

I'm attenuate of life, no light, no reverie, no hold
Vehemently trapped in my contused world
Rearward it's weird, ahead deceptive
Ensconced without inclination, bereft of confidence
Naive to conceive it cinch to beget a difference
Disenthralled I'm clueless to the next leap
Amiable to cover my head and sleep
Cognisant that I have to move, dawdling is enticing
I'm petrified of what's next

The next blow came when I visited my daughter. She welcomed me with a closed door. She locked herself in her room. Later she sent me an email which read in part, 'you never cared about me. My mom looked after me alone. You want to come back into my life, how do you think I survived until now?' It was heart rending, but I could sense a lot of influence from the mother. I hoped that one day she would be able to look at the situation with an independent mature mind. Before then it was going to be very hard. I understood her anger but I could not justify myself now. It was the most painful point in my life. To be disowned by my own child was the worst of all my plights. My world crushed around me. When the burden becomes too much and we feel we cannot carry it alone, there is always the comfort of that last resort, His door is always open, every human on this earth knows He is the ultimate sanctuary. He is God. Godmother had told me that the most powerful and simple prayer regardless of creed or religion is our Father's prayer. I knelt down and prayed,

> Our father who art in heaven, hallowed be thy name
> Thy kingdom come, thy will be done on earth as it
>   is in heaven
> Forgive us our trespasses as we forgive those who
>   trespass against us
> Give us this day our daily bread and lead us not into
>   temptation
> But deliver us from evil
> Forever and ever
> Amen

Godmother had once tipped me, 'Mbiramatako you cannot have it all in life,' I resolved to live life to the fullest and to never collect regrets. I was going to plan financial support for my daughter, and if she refused it, I would keep it for her until somehow we worked out our relationship. Whatever I wished for myself, I also wished for my daughter.

I wanted her to absorb as much knowledge from the world as possible. Knowledge was going to be her best weapon in life. Life had to go on. I intended to have joy and varied experiences that would bring me knowledge. There was a lot in the world to do to afford to sit down in despair. I tried my best to amend the hard landing into some sort of soft landing. I settled for a job in the local clinic. I put up in my childhood home, in my small boyhood bedroom. I bargained for a loan from my employer, got a modest amount and bought a 1970 Beetle Sedan. It was in good condition. I took it to a garage that specialised in vintages. I told them I wanted everything upgraded. Most importantly, the engine. I knew they could notch it up a bit and it would run like any new model, the shocks, new tyres, new sound system, new aircon system, new leather seats and a new shiny dark blue paint and slightly frosted windows. They gave me the total bill. I almost fainted. Fainting didn't solve my problem, my two sisters did. I didn't think it would cost so much. I was desperate.

I strived to at least have a soft landing back into life. I desired to do it in style even though I was broke. In the end I struck a deal with my second sister and she loaned me part of the money. The other part obviously was left to Godmother. She agreed to loan me more than I needed so that I could meet running costs. She always looked ahead. I paid half the bill. They said I can collect my car in one month and settle the rest. One month passed. The garage called me to collect my car. I felt very tense. It felt like I was going on a date. I reached and they showed me my 1970 Beetle Sedan in its new glory. They had improvised on the tyres and put what they called balloon tyres. It made the little car look luxurious. Inside it was paradise. All the padding and the seats were fitted with new leather. The sound system was exceptionally good. They put a wooden dashboard to give it a grand feel. I jumped inside. I started the engine and it immediately roared to life.

The smell of new leather and gasoline was exhilarating. I took a test drive. It was fantastic. They had put in power steering. It was smooth, no bumps, no noise, only the power of the Beetle. I paid and drove home. The Beetle became a hit with everyone who saw it. Very hard not to fall in love with it. My family were happy for me. It was a good buy. It felt funny after all these years, those experiences, to come back to this humble life like a boy again. At times memories of Mei would come. I felt as if my stomach was upset. My feelings for her were painfully strong. I felt she had cheated me of my memento mori. Deep down I knew she did everything with purpose. It was hard to have soft landing. I noticed that people were very ingenious. They did not rely on work pay. Everyone was striving to make an extra buck. I didn't want to be last like the back of the head. I wanted to lead like the nose. I quickly hatched my own side business. I got income from my job at the clinic. I used part of that income to finance a small t shirt sales shop. I took it as a hobby. I printed t shirts under the label NNUTS. It stood for nothing new under the sun. The t shirts were a hit. I quickly included leather products. I rented a corner in one supermarket. My cousin took care of things there. I was happy the supermarket boss agreed to let out the bigger space that exited out into the street. The space became my unique shop. NNUTS Collections. It had a steady following. I saw different beautiful people at the shop. Working women and men who knew what they wanted in fashion. To give my little shop character I played music on vinyl only. I had a good supply from the collection at home.

I went back from work and quickly changed my uniform. Rushed to the gate where my childhood friends were waiting sitting on the hood of the beetle. I cringed. That body work cost a lot. If I told my friend it would definitely sound rude. Off we went to the local pub. They were self employed odd job men. Sometimes they had money to buy the local brew. Sometimes it was me. This is how we grew up. When one man's beard is on fire all men will help to put it out. If one of us was broke it made no difference. Everyone will help him. I had gone back to basics. To humble wisdom that was simple and practical. The bliss of a simple life! Today it was me buying. It was a day after pay day. We went to the pub and started on the brew. When I came back I did not drink so much. I was settling back into the old lifestyle I grew up doing. No change had come. So many dreams, big dreams. In the end it all came to this local pub, noisy and filthy but comfortable. My thoughts strayed to Mei. I shook my self out of it.

I accepted the mug of brew. I thought about my work colleague. Not much had changed in my society. People were still facing simple intricacies of life. My colleague belonged to a faith sect. He was a nurse like me. Both he and his wife were devout worshippers. He represented a stable example of a marriage. His wife used to supplement the family income by trading goods from neighbouring SA and reselling in the country. My work colleague was clean. He never did promiscuous activities. We all knew that. When his penis started leaking a strange grey discharge he was dumbfounded. He didn't know what the problem was. Probably it will go away he thought. But it persisted. It became painful to urinate. His wife was away in SA. During lunch time we went to the staff canteen for food. After food people sat in a small group of friends and whiled up the remaining lunch minutes talking trivia. 'Guys my penis is coming out puss!' Everyone was silent. Our guy couldn't keep it to himself much longer. No one answered him. Silence. After a while everyone stood up and returned to work. Back in the clinic I took him aside. I told him to visit the doctor downstairs. 'But I don't have an infection. Where would I get it? I sleep with my wife only' he looked at me. I looked at him paused, urging him on. At last he got it. He stood up and went to the doctor. My thoughts were jerked back to reality by an old woman doing a dance, generally displaying drunken behaviour. I looked around me. The council bar had long benches. Adverts of a popular condom brand adorned the vast walls. I believed that these billboards had served their failed purpose. They remained an eyesore and a shameful identity especially if they happen to flash in news clips on the international media. My country is just bursting at the seams for a new identity, a new prosperity devoid of stereotypical behaviour. All countries that display moral decadence and decay reflect their leadership. Same as a bad child reflects its parents. Later we took some takeaways and went home.

As we reached home I saw a car that did not look familiar parked outside the house. I went inside the gate. I deciphered from outside the front door a delicate form sitting with my mom. I went inside. It was Mei. I couldn't believe it. I felt weak in the knees. I desperately needed a cigarette! I only managed to say weakly, 'how did you find me here?' I was sweating. I needed a seat. I sat down and looked at Mei. She looked at me. She was as beautiful as ever. Her cheeks flushed pink. I could feel her eyes scanning me. Her eyes were moist and shiny. She sat straight and graceful. Her hair was simply let down in a rich wave. Her skin was flawless. Her lips pink and pouty! I desperately needed to kiss her on her pretty lips. In my culture it's inappropriate to show affection by kissing in front of elders. 'This is my family house' I told her. At last she said 'I told you one day, in good time the 'Mbiramatako' will be priceless. Presently I'm getting offers in the 7 figures only. I'm here to personally ask if you still want the painting or you want to go for the millions.' Everyone around us, my family, my friends, did not understand what we were talking about. It was something that had the potential to dramatically change my life. Mei left to sleep at her hotel. I thought about her offer. My family's fortunes would be instantly changed if I went for the money. We could buy a new house and I could buy a farm to replace grandma Chihwiza's one. We would have plenty left. If managed well, we could live comfortably for the rest of our life! The next day I went and took three days off from work.

I drove to Mei's hotel. I planned to take her out sight seeing. She wanted us to use her rented BMW Sports car but I told her I was going to take her in my old beetle. She was surprised when she sat inside. She said 'hey this cute little baby is a real comfy hah?' she enjoyed the ride. The beetle was running exceptionally smooth, as if to show off to Mei. I put the CD, 'Here comes the sun' by the Beatles. The music enveloped us. 'You know Mei, John Lennon once said, that he was not sure which would go first, Christianity or rock and roll but he said he was quite sure the Christian faith would go away and he said the Beatles were more popular than Jesus. He also said Jesus was alright but his disciples were thick and ordinary. He said it was them twisting it that ruined it for him.' Now the song, 'I wanna hold your hand' was playing. I reached out and held Mei's small delicate hand. 'Later he was shot down and died, right?' Mei asked 'Yes' I agreed. I accelerated the little car. I headed to the biggest people's market in Mbare in the Capital. I parked the jalopy. We both got out and walked around the big market. It was a shock for her to see so many people of different colour to herself all at one time. I took her to the stall where they sell traditional healing products. Later I told Mei that I was going to drive to my uncle Tony. I needed to get a charm to make her stay and never want to leave again. She laughed. I continued, 'you know what, even if you want to go back, still you cannot because I have charmed you. The voodoo charm from my uncle, the one he mixes the intestines of the male and female lizards is very powerful.' She cut me off bursting into laughter.

We drove to an old location where I had stayed before when I was a young bachelor. This is where I had built my house years ago. She was surprised to see so many people at the shopping centre and so many bars and people publicly drinking. They all looked at her. I wanted to take her to another city where the ruins of my ancestors are located. I also wished for Mei to see the Victoria Falls. Unfortunately time was not allowing. I settled for a visual description of the two areas. I explained to Mei that the original name for the Victoria Falls was Mosi Oa Tunya, which means smoke that thunders. When David Livingstone came to my country he 'discovered' the falls. He named them Victoria Falls in honour of his queen. Mei shook her head, 'how daring to go to another man's house and name his beautiful daughter in honour of your grandmother without the parents' permission.'

From there we drove towards the capital city. I took Mei to my grandma's stolen farm and showed her from a distance all the familiar landmarks that I had told her about. The two dams and the river running through the farm were clear from where we stood. As I looked at the tall granite stone, the most sacred landmark standing majestically, I nearly cried. I controlled myself. 'You know Mei, it's oft said that whatever the consequence one day the baboon was seen climbing steep slopes when it was already dark. Normally a baboon won't do this. When something really has to be done, so it will be done. If I could get enough inspiration from someone like you I could fight for our inheritance and I could win it back. I never really fought to get this treasure back. I need a good reason to fight. Imagine what we could do with this heaven on earth of natural land? You and I could build a whole new nation out of this farm! Oh Mei, I'm in pain day and night.' After a while we drove back to the city. I left her at her hotel and went to my parents' house.

The next day I called Mei to come and spend the day with my family. She came. We prepared traditional food. I'd prepared cow's feet for her. She particularly liked it. She said it made her stomach stable. She could drink more of the fine liquor we had. My sister taught her a lot about my people's culture and beliefs. She was surprised to find common familiar beliefs between her culture and my culture. Godmother was always very creative with her hands. She designed her own attires. One particularly beautiful outfit she made, she gave it to our mother as a birthday present. It was this special outfit that my mom gave to Mei as her present. It was a traditional skirt and top but it was slightly big for Mei. I called Gushungo from next door. He came very fast sensing a quick buck. He measured Mei and took the attire with him. After 45 minutes he returned it. It was a perfect fit. I gave him his fee and looked at Mei. I caught my breath. She looked just like my mother's daughter in law. She never took it off. She looked beautiful. My mom and sister's friends came and greeted her. The house was full and everyone was singing together. Food and booze, it was splendid. Mei was surprised at how popular we were in the area.

On that day I took out my talisman. I strummed the mbira standing. Moving around the house, shaking my bald head from side to side. I was like a possessed male medium. I read in my history books about heroes like Mbuya Nehanda and Sekuru Kaguvi. I never really thought how significant they are to our pride. Playing my instrument, with the women ululating and Mei clapping her delicate hands. I felt like the spirit of Kaguvi had descended. The spirit of victory over indigenous people's problems! She danced and sang and cooked sadza, a local staple in my country and in Southern Africa. It tastes bland to those used to rice as a staple. She tried the Mopani worm but said she needed time to get used to it. In the end she told me she was sleeping at the house. Mom quickly made a room available for her with clean bedclothes and sundry. We all went to sleep with happy smiles on our faces. The next day Mei went to her hotel to prepare for her return journey. My love for the 'Mbiramatako' was equivalent to the love I had for Mei. I couldn't afford losing both. The real choice I had was the 'Mbiramatako.' As for Mei all I could do was formulate some rhyme to express and get it out. The pain,

You are cruel, Miss Mei

Your ambience flutters around my solicitude
You wriggle like a mermaid out of cincture
Volant dragonfly at the pond, hard to catch
You are celestial, a healing mystery like Stonehenge
Detached and solitary, adorable and abstruse in attitude
Denied, my heart gush, I accredit cruelty sans your nature
Euphuistic care, coruscate in the smouldering depth
    of the eye
You aren't wont to pecksniffery, it's your principle

Mei sent the painting the following month. My family saw the painting. They were surprised why I didn't take the money. I was sitting in my parents' house. I couldn't hang the 'Mbiramatako' on the wall because it was too massive for the walls of my childhood house. In the end I put it standing against the wall. It was a perfect position. I went through the old vinyl collection kept in the house. I chose Lynyrd Skynrd, 'Tuesday's Gone' I reminisced about Mei. I sat and looked at the painting which was me right there. Nude with the skull in one corner of the painting and zebra mask in my hand. It was bizarrely beautiful. Mei was correct when she said she captures fine moods and details like the schizoid's brain. The painting was nothing like I'd ever seen. It was alive. It scared visitors to the house with its beauty. Especially my mom's old friends. It always made me laugh. Inside I was wailing. I was bitter. I had gone east hoping for prosperity. I did not bring money or car. I brought my mask from grandma Chihwiza, my gold pendant from Alex and the darling of my life, the 'Mbiramatako.' I was poor and was wealthy. I felt Mei right there in the room. That was the main reason I would never let go of that painting. Wherever I go I will take it with me. Mei is always with me. Although I won't instruct it, still I know that they will put the 'Mbiramatako' at the head of my beautiful casket when I go on the Grand journey.

A few local crooks became excited when they first saw Mei. A month later a courier service company bearing something that looked expensive. Soon they all knew I had something in my house worth breaking in for. In my country burglaries are a major nuisance. One night they burgled and tried to steal the 'Mbiramatako.' I was in deep slumber. The moment the shadow of the thief hit the painting I was up as if by set alarm. I jumped up screaming 'thief! thief. The thieves ran away without taking anything. I bought a spear and planted it next to the 'Mbiramatako.' I declared, 'any one who dares to come into our house and try to be malicious. I'm going to spear him like I would an animal in the hunt. I will protect my 'Mbiramatako.'

The month of May had come upon us. It was cold especially in the morning. I was waiting for transport to go to work. The beetle was at the garage for maintenance. It was 6 am. The cool breeze of May breathed Mei's memory to me and enveloped me in nostalgic reflection. God I loved that woman. I always thought of her. At least I had the 'Mbiramatako' to remind me of her. I remembered her nimble feet as we danced barefoot in that apartment in China.

Oh Mei

Oh Mei, you impressed as no woman has ever
I adulate with my essence, not my oblong
Proximal, yet so abroad you sealed it with never
I try to obliterate, conceivably be free of memory
Of one so ambrosial, imperturbable, so merry
Am I to die of despair? Lord of mercy
Accord me instant amnesia, total anamnesis
Of Mei, the ensemble

As this sad rhyme played in my mind I became oblivious to everything around me. I was as good as sleep walking. I didn't notice the young man riding his bike with a huge pile of newspapers strapped to the bike. He was riding very fast despite his load. The instant I noticed him the impact happened. It was very fast. I flew backwards with newspapers following me and eventually the heavy thud on top of me. It was the young man. His weight almost knocked me out. Soon the morning workers gathered around and helped us. They all had a good laugh after they saw I was not hurt. My work uniform was less lucky than me. It was in tatters. I went back home to change. As I reached the house I felt sudden dizziness. Before I could hurry inside I fell down and slipped into a deep sleep. I was later told that mom took me to hospital and fortunately it was just a concussion. No wonder Godmother had come back. She thought I was in very serious condition. She was always there in crises to help.

Meanwhile in China, Mei's sharp mind was restless. She felt that something was amiss. She just could not place it. Since coming back from Mbiramatako's country she felt emptiness. A yearning for something different, exotic and long lasting. She shivered. Her face set serious, she paced around the lounge. She went and threw herself in the sofa. She sighed. She took her flute and started a sweet sorrowful, wailing flute. She drifted off in sad slumber. As she slowly woke up she tried to cling to the dream. She was telling someone she didn't see or recognize to 'please stop playing 'The beautiful bride' it scares me . . .' she was awake, startled to see saliva had drippled down her lovely cheek. 'God I didn't realise I went out flat. That dream was very scary!' she thought to herself. She stood and tiptoed into the kitchen to fix something to eat. She didn't like the dream at all, it had sinister connotations. She felt a premonition, a great anxiety and fear. 'I hope Mbiramatako is alright' her mind wandered. She was not sure why she had thought of him. For the next moments Mei toyed around with an idea, she flipped it over in her curious brain, played hide and seeks with it. She was a very careful woman. She never made a move without first weighing all sides.

After a few more thoughts she rested. She went to take a shower. As she dried herself it suddenly hit her. What she had been trying to deny to herself was simple. At last, to her utter disbelief, she had fallen in love. She decided to confront herself. In the end she made a startling decision. Her mind became active. She knew the implication of marriage to Mbiramatako. She was glad she had exposed Mbiramatako to true love. He can explain to his people. She had not given in to Mbiramatako's sexual advances but she was hopelessly attracted. Mei anticipated the momentous occasion when she would finally present herself to him. It was going to be more special because it was going to be done in his country. He intimated to her that his people still practiced an old custom whereby a new bride had to be tested for virginity. He told her that on the first night the new couple had sex they used a new clean white cloth under their bodies when they had intercourse. In the morning the elderly aunts would collect it and see if there was human virgin blood. An in law who passed this test was proud and comfortable in the family. Her stance not to have sex with a man was going to pay off. Mbiramatako was going to have a full boat. She looked at her slim figure in the wall mirror and smiled mischievously to herself. She was going to Mbiramatako. She had made up her mind. Mei could not stand to delay anymore. She informed Vlarena of her decision. She told her that later she would come back with Mbiramatako to formalise issues with the parents. Vlarena knew she could not stop Mei.

I awoke and I felt someone holding my hand. It was my sister. Godmother. Whenever Godmother visited the family home she rummages the vinyl collection. She fishes out her favourite, Ray Charles and Willie Nelson, 'Seven Spanish Angels.' The song was playing in low volume in the background. The moment I heard that song I knew Godmother was around. No one else played that song. I looked up at the familiar asbestos roof inside my old family home and turned to her. She looked into my eyes. She did not say anything. She could read me like a book. She only, understood the anguish that was eating me up. It was not the paper boy and his racing bike or the concussion. It simply was Mei. Godmother felt helpless. She was not sure if the woman I referred to as Mei would ever come back again. She was not even sure if the woman loved me. She could tell I had something to say. She leaned closer. I said, 'take care of the 'Mbiramatako' I began to cry silently. Bitter painful cry proudly held in check. The emotions finally won and I lost it. I wept like a small baby. My whole body shook with emotion.

Godmother did not say anything. She rocked me softly. The rocking lulled me into momentary deep slumber. I'm not sure how long I snoozed. I began to feel as if some very heavy weight was pressing upon my body. I struggled. The heaviness started to settle around my ribcage. It pressed down slowly but surely. I couldn't breathe. I tried to struggle but couldn't move. I tried to scream.

No words came out! I began to say Jesus, Jesus, repeatedly. Slowly the dead weight lifted off, I felt relief. I opened my eyes. I beheld a flower. I promptly leapt out of bed and flung myself into her open delicate arms. Embracing her full in my own. Her fresh scent wafted into my nostrils strong. I hugged her closer and she gathered me closer. We both stood motionless. I felt crushing pain, a rare pain that may be best described in terms of the unique pain of giving child birth. Words limit me. All my joints felt weak. I hung on to Mei. My brain felt like it was going to burst. I bubbled into the most brilliant soft light, a light of happiness, I couldn't see, I felt Mei very close. Every minute breath I felt it. She raised my tear stained face and kissed me on the lips. She cried out with raw emotion and gripped me closer. We swayed in a very slow dance as 'Seven Spanish Angels' slowly came to conclusion in the background. We held on in each other's arms, with Godmother watching, smiling at us. Everything in the room became smaller and smaller to eventual invisibility to me. The two of us felt like we were bloating into a bubble. I couldn't feel us. Only the sway remained.

Ode to Miss Mei

Swain yonder sin
Ingenerate upon in May,
Moonstruck by the mistral of May,
I relish a walk,
To strike Mei in the park,
Selfsame mirage, Mei sojourn an elusive dove
Precisely poignant hence twain discern love
Parched up, I rash for a wintry whiff of May
Ceaseless enchanting adumbrates and seeks
Vex me to the skirts of seppuku

I hunch a crush lustrous, proximate I discern it askance
I'm shackled, dangling on a rope of hope
Seduced by mutual allure, both play and hop
Persevering as natural to nature, Mei lugs on,
I commit my hand to her, hers she giveth not
Subtle and silent, consistent as the glowing sun
She won't ante up a sign, the play is pain

Inconversant consequence,
She run, I yearn
Mei is mean
Is it innate to obsess for It?
Is it inherent in Man to seek an unparalleled love?
Is Mei the epitome of chocolate full of Ricin?
I fear her, I abhor dying without the Lantern
Dreadful heart afflicts the body, eat it up with disease
Conceivably I relinquish of painful heart,
Nevermore to see Mei

I distress loss of the percipience
Rendered ethereal, sensitive as a raw wound
Subjugated by an intense melancholy confused
I'm susceptible to Mei, I do the string dance
I mind not one beat
My psyche, benevolence, wealth, haul all
Seize entirety, preserve one of all,
Mei
I inaugurate in her soul

I crave Mei for the entrada
God unbidden in the actual, the key to carry forth
Godmother abiding, I immerse in her bosom of comfort
Close my eyes to pain feasibly to dream oft
Mei

I know that I know nothing,
Inanity to go on a trip that left me high and tripping?
What should I emulate? Should I poise forlorn, like
    the weed in the river?
Appalled to my roots by Mei, I'm now a man without
    Religion,
Without sin

I pine her in the extant phenomenon and looming
Grander happening
Some in conjecture, in dire dread
Endeavour to be exquisite, apt for the Grand journey
Others bawl,
I simper in celebratory howl
At the culmination, Mei has become with me
Mei pellucid the temptation maze
Of evil and good, putrefaction and pleasure
Mei with me, I fear not the winter of June

REFERENCES

http://www.historyorb.com/events/date/1976?p=5

http://www.youtube.com